I0843489

BLAME IT ON NIKKI

by Teresa Wasson

Copyright © 2025 by – Teresa Wasson – All Rights Reserved.

It is not legal to reproduce, duplicate, or transmit any part of this document in either electronic means or printed format. Recording of this publication is strictly prohibited.

Disclaimer

This book is a work of fiction. The characters, incidents, places, events, and dialogue are drawn from the author's imagination and are not to be construed as real. Any resemblance to actual persons, living or dead, is entirely coincidental.

Table of Contents

Dedication

This book is dedicated to my sons. They have watched me grow as I have watched them grow. We remain loyal as a unit and celebrate our successes. There's no success without trials and we had our share. We continue to encourage and uplift each other throughout.

The soil which you tiller is rich! You must dig deep enough to uncover your mineral.

~Karika Atman

About the Author

Teresa Wasson is a Legal Secretary and avid reader of all genres. She has been employed with government agencies for over twenty years. Teresa studied literature at Eastern Michigan University in 1994 and holds a bachelor's degree in business management. It was during this time she uncovered her ability to take current events and use satirical comedy to change the ending of the story. Captivating her classmates and her audience with fictional stories that sounded believable, only to tell them she was just kidding around. She used the technique to encourage laughter and thought-provoking discussions, which has been an integral component in raising her two sons. Writing is her first love. She enjoys sharing life experiences and finding humor throughout all the adversity life has brought her. Laughter is medicine to her soul. Positive therapeutic self-care is a must for Teresa. Aside from her day job, Teresa is a professional entrepreneur and the co-owner of a luxury online candle business. She enjoys roller skating, traveling, and good conversation with friends and family.

Acknowledgements

I would like to thank my supportive family. Family is not just blood relations. Family is those who surround themselves around you and are there with you for the highs and lows of life. I want to thank anyone who was a personal inspiration in writing this book, especially victims of domestic abuse. Whether it was emotional or physical wounds inflicted by a parent, spouse, or significant other, the ultimate reward is healing. Healing is personal and what that looks like for every individual is something different. I would like to thank my readers and those of you who listened to my fictional stories daily. I appreciate the ears who listened as I walked into work to tell "my version" of a story, providing nine-to-five entertainment. I finally put my voice on paper.

Prologue

The definition of magic- the power to influence the course of events by using mysterious or supernatural forces. There are several categories of tricks a magician will perform. Some of those tricks fall into these categories:

- Vanish- A disappearing act where the subject reappears.
- Production- Producing something out of nothing
- Transformation-Changing usual appearance, morphing
- Penetration- Making objects appear to pass through one another
- Restoration-Returning damaged objects to an optimal state
- Levitation-Making something rise to the air without support
- Attraction-Rituals or spells to bring someone closer to you
- Sympathetic Reaction-symbolic ordering of the world, disparate objects and ideas can have unexpected correspondences and new potential
- Invulnerability- defying odds
- Physical Anomaly-turning one thing into something else
- Spectator Failure- Misguiding the audience
- Control-Who gets to use an object in the game
- Identification-Ability to identify magic and learn how to use it
- Prediction-Cold reading, make educated guesses
- Extra-sensory perception-the idea that people can perceive the world through a means other than the five senses, also known as the sixth sense

A person will have an introduction to or experience magic, either in their childhood or adult life. Magic can have various effects on one's mental psyche. The magician's goal is to successfully perform a trick that will leave the audience with one or two outcomes, awestruck or fascinated. Unfortunately, a novice magician will have the opposite effect on their audience, leaving the audience confused and disappointed.

Tactlessly, manipulation and illusion are components of the art of magic, practiced by Maleeky Richard. His friends called him Dick for short. He was also known as Mr. Magic "Dick", a well-known handyman who owned Mr. Magic's Restorations in the City of Hangtown. Mr. Magic was also an investor in small businesses. His infamous love bomb act was about to force Detective Nikki Harris to highlight her performance. Mr. Magic's encore with Nikki would make him the subject of a vanishing trick that stunned the crime-ridden streets of Hangtown, Michigan.

1

INTRODUCTION

I always knew there was something different about me. Not the kind of difference that was obvious to the average eye. Looking at me, you would suppose I was the typical girl raised in a middle-class family, and I was. My difference was on the inside. I felt something was missing or taken away. Sometimes, there was a feeling that I was a different person than I was supposed to be. I likened it to knowing we are born with two feet for balance, but if you are born with one, you adapt and go with the flow. That's what I do: go with the flow. You will learn to balance without having the other foot. I was born with all my appendages. I'm anatomically correct, but there was a part of me missing that wasn't uncovered until later in my adult life. My physical features stood out. Standing five feet & ten inches tall-flat, cocoa complexion, with long coarse hair, which drapes the middle of my back, was just a tiny bit of what I thought was different. Little did I know, everyone but me knew what one of those differences was. The man I know as dad, Benny Harris, is not my biological father. Benny, not being my biological father, was obvious. One of these things is not quite like the other.

My stepfather, Benny Harris, was inherently a father figure. I say inherent because he was my mother's husband. Due to my mother and Benny being married at the time of my birth, I assumed his last name. Benny was not much of an affectionate father. Although he showed me basic things, he was not much of a life coach either. I can say he was an excellent provider for my mother and my siblings. I benefited from his provisions by being a part of the pack. The things I learned from him were through observation. Observation became a strategy for me to familiarize myself with the unknown. Early on, my observations of Benny helped me realize I do not ever marry a philandering alcoholic. Confused and anguished, all in the same ball of emotions, discovering Benny was not my father was not the worst that could happen. It was all the little lies and the deception that preceded the revelation, making me feel I would be on an endless journey of uncovering dark secrets and untruths. Hence, the reason I became a detective.

I have two sisters. Celeste and Wendy. Our two southern parents migrated to the North and settled in Downriver, Michigan, raising us in the City of Hangtown. The area was a hidden gem. A tight-knit community where everyone knew everyone. If you did not know them, your mother or father knew something about them. The community is diverse and has been for some time. I am in no rush to leave Hangtown. Hangtown may want me to leave once they discover how different this five-foot-ten, one hundred-and-seventy-pound, slender girl is.

2

SISTER MAGIC

I love that despite the obvious that my sisters and I are half-siblings, we are a whole force together. We communicate regularly. Sometimes, our conversations are about nothing. We share our deepest thoughts and even talk about our sexual escapades. My sisters labeled me the shock factor queen. My style of things is a matter of fact, with all the juicy and gory details. It was no fun leaving things to the imagination. As far as my personal life goes, it was my tea to spill out to my sisters. I did just that. When it came to police work, I used discretion.

When they say birth order matters, it does. Celeste is the middle sibling; she suffers from Middle Child Syndrome. There is a year between us. Celeste is a bit of a melodramatic supporting actor to me. As a kid, Celeste kept the bullies away from her scrawny baby sister, me, Nikki. Celeste avoided trouble but had a thing for rough-around-the-collar kind of men. She is married to Keith. After spending fifteen years in federal prison, Keith met Celeste and became a pastor of a church in Texas. They have three children together. Keith and Celeste have two sons and a daughter, Kam'ron. Celeste like to call me out on my bull shit. I like to call her out on hers. We would fuss, but not for long. If she knew what I got myself into as of late, she would crap out bricks.

Then there's Wendy, Wen for short; she is the oldest. She is five years older than me. Wendy is married to Rod. She is business oriented and so is Rod. Like me, they are kid-free. They opted for a child-free life. Although, I always wanted to be a mother. We are all grown up and living in different states. Celeste lives in Texas, and Wendy lives in Florida. I am a true Michiganian and would not dream of leaving my "blue" family. I established my career as a police officer when I was twenty-one. Fifteen years later, I am still fond of the work. It is rewarding. Stressful at times but rewarding. Outside of the contractual benefits, being an officer has served me well.

Even though I am well over thirty, Celeste and Wendy check on me frequently. Their check-ins are genuinely about my safety. On the streets of Hangtown, an officer's chances of going home without injury or alive were becoming slim to none. Crime is up, and respect for an officer is at an all-time low. Community morale is suffering. I supposed that is why Celeste and Wen hot-tailed it out of Michigan.

To keep them from worrying about me daily, I gave them courtesy calls. My sisters also had concerns about me living my life on the edge and doing so with unsavory characters. No doubt, they want to hear about the latest tea on the cases I was working on. Especially the ones about old neighborhood friends. My sister was more interested in keeping up with her ex-boyfriend, Lou. Lou had taken her to the prom ages ago. He married three times since he dated Wendy and divorced three times, too. She always says, Lou would have been better off living the Bachelor's life. He ran an illegal swinger's club. In which I had the pleasure of investigating. It was a clean operation, but there were concerns that there were underage participants. Anytime his spot was raided, it was for selling alcoholic beverages without a license. No underage persons were caught there. When it came to Celeste inquiring about her ex, Clay, I was tight-lipped. Celeste was head over heels for Clay. They had a puppy love. Clay was now married to Celeste's old friend. Any information given to her about Clay, she took it personally. Everything that went wrong in his life was the direct result of karma. The karma he was catching for marrying her friend. So, I would bounce right over the subject.

I did not mind sharing with them. I keep much of the details out to protect the innocent, and my job but deliver the story to them as if they were right in the middle of the action. I was not ready to divulge to them there was going to be a high-profile case hitting the news soon. People they are familiar with are the subject. If I do not tell them first, the news will surely send shock through their veins. Before sharing any details with them, I must check the leads on the case.

3

BONE

Just as I was ready to sign off from work and call Celeste and Wendy, my phone rang. Looking at the caller's I.D., I initially thought it was a spam caller. My work cell contacts did not have the number saved in the contacts list. The number, *248-888-2222,* did not look familiar. 313 and 248 are codes of Detroit and surrounding areas. The area code gave me a hint to the registered location of the phone. I started not to answer. Something told me not to answer. I answered it anyway, "Detective Harris, speaking." The voice was familiar but was not catching my memory bank, "Hey, Nikki." Now I had to play guess who. The deep, raspy, congested voice was a mystery. Judging by the fact that this person has my work line and knows me by first name, assumably, it must be a newbie on the force. A newbie looking for guidance, "Who's speaking? How may I help you?"

"Nikki, this Bone. I need to talk to you in person." Bone, known on the streets of Detroit and other cities as T-Bone, is my old friend. Celeste's husband, Keith and Wendy's husband, Rod, were next-door neighbors to Bone when we were growing up. Bone and I became more than friends soon after my divorce. We knew each other before I met my then-husband. Thanks to me, Bone was a reformed criminal. At least in appearance, he was; if there was a crime to be committed, Bone was committing it. He did not discriminate against misdemeanors, felonies, white collar, petty, whatever. Bone is the guy you keep in your repertoire. You never know when you will need a guy like Bone hanging around. He was dependable. He escaped prison time after I showed him how to clean up his act.

My preference is shorter men. Bone was slightly taller than the five-foot-nothing, tall men whom I attracted. There is always a short man approaching me. Thinking he can climb the tree of life and wrap my long legs around his trunk. Bone had an appeal about him that sucked me in like a Kirby vacuum cleaner. Annoyed by his call on my work phone, I asked, "Bone, what's up, and why are you calling me on my work number?" He was slow to answer, so I figured it must be something serious or he was going to give me an anonymous tip on a case I had been working on. Why else would he choose to call my work line? The exchange on my cell phone did not record. The inside desk lines recorded all calls. The department-issued cell phones had the capability to record incoming calls if the operator of the line chose to record. The police department details and itemizes all calls. Bone calling me was going to show up somewhere. Prayerfully, it would not have to. Then I thought about it. He is calling me from a burner phone, which explains why a name did not pop up on the caller ID. Bone's voice quivered, "Let's sit down face to face and talk." Something was really upsetting him.

I hope he did not get himself into a pile of crap that would land us both in prison. I do not know if it is a good thing or not, but Bone and I have a history. We have things in common. Exposing those commonalities could be detrimental for us both. Reluctantly responding to his request to meet up, "Okay, you want to meet up today for dinner at my place." I swear I wish I had not answered the phone. Bone spoke eagerly, "Yeah, that is cool. I will be there about seven." This was the first time I ever heard T-Bone sound so uneasy. I tried to lighten him up, "Nigha, you know I don't eat after six." Without hesitation, he wittily responded, "Girl, you have been eating this dick after six since I met you." Now, that was the familiar, covert, arrogant undocumented felon talking. I gave him a time to meet me at my house, using my baby talk voice, "See you at seven, bye… my little undocumented felon." I referred to Bone as an undocumented felon because he has never been caught committing a felony crime, but everyone knew what he did for a living.

There was no use trying to muse over what he wanted. I figure he is trying to get me to help someone he knows out of their garbage. Bone thinks of me as the fixer. He is the one person who really knows me and knows what I am capable of. Sometimes, I surprise myself with the things I will do. I have another side to my personality. T-Bone is the only person alive who knows about the other side.

I hope what he wants to discuss does not require me, sweet Nikki, to morph into the other side of my personality… *Angel.* The name *Angel* is a total oxymoron to the personality. When Nikki's *Angel* shows up, things get ugly quickly. It gets so ugly; it scares me to think about it.

I better give my sisters a call before I forget to make my bi-weekly "tea-spilling" call. Whenever I have an impromptu meeting with Bone, they are the first to know. When Bone and I get together, things get haywire. When we were kids, we came up with the ingenious idea to set the neighborhood firefighter's trash bin on fire just for kicks and giggles. My thoughts were starting to run rampant, imagining what he wanted to talk about; and of course, the phone wanted to act up.

It would be so much easier to connect my Bluetooth inside the car. Paranoia keeps me from doing it, though. The idea of *Big Brother* in the car agitates my soul. The irony of being a detective and not wanting to be surveilled. If I call Celeste first, she will merge Wendy into the call. I will not have to worry about doing all of that. I will dial Celeste first and put her on the speakerphone, and she will manage the rest.

#2

Sitting my hot cocoa in the console of my black 2015 BMW 3 Series, the call connected, "Hey, you happy hooker, how's my Little *angel,* Kam'ron?" Happy hooker was my nickname for Celeste because she was far from being one. Celeste was saved by grace and sanctified by God. Happy to be the first lady of a church. I asked about Kam'ron the most. My niece Kam'ron reminded me of myself, not because she looks nothing like Keith, her father, but because Kam'ron had a feisty side to her personality.

With a bothersome mood, Celeste greeted me with, "What's going on, Nikki? What are you up to?" As I expected, she wasted no time dialing Wen. We were all merged on the call, "How's the heat treating y'all nappy hair?" The heat in Texas and Florida was too much for me.

That was another reason Michigan became the place I decided on as my permanent residency. Wen obnoxiously loud, "Girllll bye, you the only one with nappy hair. I know you wish our daddy were yours. You would not have to worry about those kinks on your neck." We all laughed. I perceived Wendy meant no harm, but finding out the man who raised me was not my father at the age of twenty was a source of contention. My identity, as I knew it, was snatched from me. People told me to chalk it up. I didn't understand what that was supposed to be. Yeah, life goes on, but who am I in this life?

I always managed to get through the side jokes. But the betrayal I felt from my mother was a deep wound that most would never understand. I despised betrayal. Wendy could sense in my fake half of laugh, laugh; the jokes were becoming stale. "Nikki, you know I am just fucking with you. What is going on in Michigan?" Before my sisters could squeeze out any more bastard baby jokes, I eased my anticipated meeting with Bone into the conversation. "Guess who's coming for dinner?" They had no time to guess. Blurting out, "Bone… Bone is coming over. He wants to discuss something. Not sure about what, but he may want me to lose evidence for him or a friend. Bone just might want me to lose my panties." Me speaking about Bone gets Celeste so worked up. It was a part of her protective nature.

Celeste, with her dramatic surge, "Damn Nikki, you are going to end up on the other side of the law if you don't stop fixing shit!" I waited for Wendy to chime in. Assuming she would not, considering all the things I fixed for her husband. The only response from Wendy was a dry "Unnnhuhhh." Wendy was less theatrical. It wasn't that she did not care, but Wen had to run her business and keep an eye on Rod, too. Rod was a traveling man. Wendy was always packing suitcases and picking clothes up from the cleaners. She was happy to do it, too. Especially since Rod had her driving an Infiniti-Q60. Wendy's lack of input did not mean she did not share the same opinion as Celeste. Frankly, being a *fixer* bought my niece and nephews nice gifts.

I could care less about what they thought about my side jobs on the job. Being an officer does not pay enough, especially after losing income from my divorce. Heck, if I had children, I would struggle to maintain the lifestyle I have for myself now.

"Anyways, Celeste and Wen, hope you all have a good day, just wanted to check in before I go ride this pony." Wen' jumped on that comment, "I thought y'all was going to be discussing something. You ain't said nothing about jumping Bone's bone. Nikki do not mess around and make that man your future ex-husband." It was remarks like that that made me love talking with my sisters. *My future ex-husband.* They think they know me. It was no secret I never really wanted to get married. I enjoyed commitment and exclusiveness, but there was something about being married that felt smothering. My mantra: trust no one! Who knows, I probably had not found the one that I wanted to compromise and share my life with. We laughed before ending the call with I love you.

4

STREET MAGIC

The good thing about working for Hangtown, I was not too far from home. I was far enough away to keep the civilians from knowing I was hiding in plain sight. Not so far that it would take me hours to get home and unwind. Time was on my side, and I had a chance to unwind before Bone came through. Something about that guy's immaculate style of dress and smooth bronze complexion kept me infatuated. Bone did not have me so infatuated that I felt the need to slip on anything sexy for his arrival. We were close. I saw him in his good days and at his worst. Oddly, Bone was not what I considered a friend. He was a comfort to me. We were used to each other. Bone viewed me the same way I viewed him. We were loyal in keeping the worst side of our character hidden from the rest of the world. Sadly, behind closed doors, Bone and I got to see the worst in each other. Bone had a way of bringing the *Angel* out of me. My fascination for him and living on the edge kept us bonded. The villain in us kept us bonded. You could say we are trauma-bonded. His lens of me was more as a trusted confidant. T-Bone was a partner in crime and a fun time!

I had time to whip something up before our tete-a-tete. It was only five-thirty in the evening. I told him seven o'clock. If I know him correctly, he will be here at six-thirty on the dot. I was thinking of cooking salmon croquettes and rice. At least, that is what I had a taste for when I was on the clock. Bone was not too fond of the fishy smell. He dreaded the odor in his Brooke's Brother's button-up shirts. Such a classic man; look for an unorthodox guy. So, stir-fry it will be! Before I could pull the wok out my mother gave me, I heard my front door creaking open. I know this predictably; unpredictable nigha did not just make it here a whole hour and a half early. Yep! He sure did. "T-Bone, is that you?"

As if we had not spoken earlier, Bone spoke with enthusiasm, "Hey, Hey…Nikki! Sweetheart, how are you? How are your mother and sisters?" *Sweetheart* was his pet- name for any woman with all her body parts. I gave Bone the look. The look as if a dead rat had surfaced in the middle of my living room floor. The look wasn't because he called me Sweetheart. The look was because Bone knew I did not talk to my mother. I love her, and I just do it from a distance. My heart wanted to forgive my mother, Terry, but *Angel* was not so forgiving. "Now you know I have not talked to Terry since 2011, but Terry is fine. Celeste and Wen stay in touch with her, so she is okay. I spoke with them earlier; all is well with them, too." His facial expression said he was shocked that I had not spoken with Terry in over five years. Whenever I was in an unmarked vehicle on official duty, I rode past her house. Getting glimpses of her, the taste of vinegar would rise to my throat and keep me from stopping. It was best if I stayed away because of the level of respect I have for my mother. I did not want to ruin it by speaking any ill words to her.

He ruined my appetite. I scratched the plan to feed him and myself, for that matter. I wanted him to spill the tea or whatever he wanted to talk about. "Why are you here? What is so important that you must show up an hour and a half earlier than scheduled? Unless you have something good to say, like you are going to run me the money you owe me for the work I put in for you, then exit through the same door entered." Bone knows when I am serious. Once he mentioned my mother, he sent my anxiety through the roof. He knows my triggers, and the thought of Terry is one of them.

Besides, he really does owe me money. Every time one of his henchmen gets caught with dope in their ride, I make a call to the evidence tech, and somehow the evidence walks out of the lockup. Bone was talking in circles and beating around the bush. I like the straightforward, direct approach to communication. It minimizes a person's inclination to lie. Say what you have to say and get it over with. The more he prolongs it, the more he will exaggerate or forget something vital. Giving him a push, "Bone, spit the shit out."

"Alright, Nikki, calm down and give me some sugar." Bone wanted a kiss, but it was prime time to display my quick wit, "Boy, look in the cabinet. I cannot believe you came over here for some sugar. I could've cash app'd you ten dollars for a store run." He unpuckered his lips and burst into a hysterical laugh, "Good one, Nikki. Now let's see if you have that same energy after I tell you about how the streets are talking." Bone knows darn well saying the streets are talking does not phase me one little bit. Who the streets are talking about and what the streets are talking about is what sparks my attention. "So, who on the streets is talking about what on the streets?" His eyes gleamed over me. Giving me a once over before pulling me close to him. The hint of Creed cologne was lightly dusted on his neck. I sniffed him so hard that I let out a snort. We did not try to hold back the laughs, "Hold up, lil' piggy", Bone pushed me away, but I was still sniffing his cologne.

Before I could finish laughing and basking in the afterglow of his scent, Bone whispered in my ear, "Old boy off Winston Dr." In Doberman Pinscher fashion, my ears perked up as if I was listening for an intruder. He could say less. I was fully aware of who Bone was talking about. Although I want to know exactly what the streets are saying. The job done on "Old Boy" was cleaner than the clothes he sent to the cleaners. It was so clean. *Angel* or I do not know how the scene got so spotless!

I leaned into Bone's embrace and felt the nibble on my ear. Somehow, when we saw each other, we succumbed to the temptations of our flesh. Our superficial infatuation for each other ran deep. Deeper than the Detroit River! Bone is not good for me. He is not good for *Angel*. I had to get him back on track, "So what's the word?" Bone never revealed sources. However, his sources were always dependable. If he said the streets are talking, then they are talking.

Pretending to use a British accent, "Well Nikki, people are questioning why "Mr. Magic" mysteriously came up missing. He vanished right before the community's eyes. Some of his family had been stomping ground asking questions about who is the cop with which he was fucking! And that would be you, my love." Bone pulled me back into his arms and we looked each other square in the eyes. I am sure mine were bucking out of my head. "Okay, and so what? I messed around with him on and off for a year or so. I am not working on the case because I revealed that to my commander. That is no secret. I ain't worried about it." I really am not worried about it. I repeated the words to myself: *I am not worried about it.* I am not ok and yes, I am worried about it. Not too many people knew Maleeky Richard and I were fooling around. It wasn't classified information. It just wasn't common knowledge in Hangtown. At least, I did not think it was.

Why on God's green earth did saying *I was not worried about it* give Bone an erection? I will never know. But it did. Life in the streets gave him a thrill, and having a lady burn both ends of the candle wick gave him an even bigger thrill. I had to keep my focus on what the plan was. Ear hustling around the precinct is the plan; see if the detectives received any plausible leads and tips. "Bone, you can leave now. I have my work cut out for me." He gently pushed away from me, adjusting the monster-size python in his grey sweats. The more he pushed away, the more I leaned in for a kiss on those plush, full lips. We both knew it was best to step away. We have a gigantic fish to deep fry. As soon as he walked through the door, I rushed to the window to watch him pull off in his pimped-out black 1983 Grand National. The car did not fit his style of dress, but it fit his persona.

I backed away from the window and prepared for a long day at work. My head stayed on swivel, and I hardly got a peaceful night's rest since that night a few years ago when Bone tried to kill me! Bone tried to kill me. Now, I must be more vigilant and look out for Magic's family. I knew very little about his family; anyone approaching me would be a suspect.

5

TRANSFORMATION MAGIC

I sipped a glass of wine every night before going to sleep. One glass a night. It was the only way my mind would find peace after October 30th, 2016. October 30th was considered Angel's Night instead of Devil's Night. Changing the name was a campaign attempt to deter destructive behavior before Halloween. I loved Halloween until then. That was the night my life would change forever. It was difficult to explain how I lost an identity when I was twenty years old, but I had gained an identity to fill the something is missing void I felt well before the age of twenty.

I laid down so that I could brainstorm the ideas of how to unofficially investigate the Mr. Magic case, my mind drifted to the dreadful Angel's Night. The events were inconceivable. No one would phantom the mayhem that occurred. That is when Bone realizes who Nikki/*Angel* really is. He has seen me in action but never against him.

He fucked around and found out! Bone is a jealous man, which is why we could never hit it off with our relationship. My family never approved of us dating, even before I started dating my ex-husband. Bone was known as a kingpin. When we were only friends, he showed his jealousy. I thought it was sweet then. Not so much now. I never witnessed him being violent. I always prayed for him to become a better man. I, too, wanted to be a better woman, morally speaking. People sell drugs for greed; some people sell drugs for need. Bone sold drugs for need. His parents had gambling and substance abuse addictions, which kept Bone and his siblings fending for themselves. He would come to our house to eat, and I would sneak him a plate outside my bedroom window. I tried not to judge him. Bone was smart. He was good at converting the metric system, ounces to pounds and adding up the money. He dropped out of school in the twelfth grade. I encouraged him to go back and even get a skilled trade. I believe most people have done something that would have them sentenced to prison, if not death, including me. I was not the only one in uniform escaping the long arm of the law. I was the one the law could not reach. Our life together would change forever after Angel's Night.

It was a long night of stopping petty crimes like vandalism and destruction of property. I made it home safely. Bone made it to the house before I arrived. He was watching television. The volume on the TV was so loud I wondered how he could even sit there in front of it. He did not cook, and I had no plans to cook or buy dinner. Seeing him there irritated me. Bone had one excuse after the other. He was not a felon on paper. You cannot boost your employer's equipment and think they are going to retain you as an employee. Heck, they could even fully prosecute his ass. Without my assistance, he always seems to manage to get out of being prosecuted. I'd imagine it's the slick talk he does. He was very cunning and manipulative. He learned to be that way early in life. Bone thought the world owed him everything because he was dealt a bad hand. In some ways, I allowed him to project that onto me and guilt me into being his person. Little did he know I felt the world owed me too.

In any case I could not allow him to think he was going to ride my back as he crossed over to living a legitimate lifestyle. He had to face the world and become his own man. My thoughts of resentment were becoming evident. I took my shower, with my stomach growling from hunger, and went straight to my room. We were in separate rooms at this point. I closed the bedroom door. It was my sanctuary. My place of peace after facing a bunch of angry people on a daily basis.

Bone interrupted my peace by storming through the door, "Do you love him!" I did not pause with my response, my voice was strong, with a serious conviction, "Get the hell out of my room acting and talking crazy." He shouted again, "Do you love him!" Again, in the calmest voice I could use, "Love who Bone?" He had a look in his eyes, which made me position myself for combat. I kept my service weapon locked up, but I slept with my 9mm pistol. That was my protection from the outside world. I never thought I would have to use it on someone in my home that I connected with.

Screaming and raging, "That mother fucker you call your partner, the simp bitch who been dropping a dime to my employer. You know who I am talking about. The little pussy you have been cracking your legs open for, for the past six months. That is who. DO YOU LOVE HIM, NIKKI?" I could tell that night was going to be a nightmare. One that either of us may never recover from. The thoughts of my mother, my sisters, my nephews, and my niece were all flashing before my eyes. Was this going to be a murder-suicide? Was this going to be a murder, and one of us fled? The television was so loud, will the neighbors even hear the commotion? Did he turn the television up so he could cover up hurting me? Did he plan this ridiculous confrontation? The more I thought about it, the angrier I became. I was no longer seeing him as poor Bone from around the block. He was not the Bone I had slept with for years. He was a disrespectful nigha off the streets, and I was going to have to show him that's exactly what I think of him.

6

PENETRATION MAGIC

What is happening? Using my training and negotiating skills, it was best not to be dismissive of his accusations. Instinctively feeling only one of us will come out alive. My gut began to stir up and ball up into knots. Words will never describe what my body was feeling. My mind was so detached from reality I could not focus on who Bone was to me. I had to focus on what he was trying to do to me. So, I stood up, hoping I could talk sense into him. Before I could plant my feet on the floor, Bone had backed hand me so hard that I could feel blood running down my chin. The force of the blow was so forceful it split my lip, and my tooth was loose. A warm sensation was running down my leg. This mother fucker knocked the piss out of me. I fell back onto the bed. With no words, I reached for my gun before getting a grip on my pistol. Bone straddled across me. His butt was sitting on my stomach. Breathless from the struggle, I pleaded for him to handle it rationally. He continued holding my weapon on me. He pressed the gun to my already busted lip and slid the nozzle down my throat. With his finger on the trigger, "Is this how you suck on his dick?" Afraid to speak, a teardrop rolled from one eye. I lost focus as images from my childhood, family, and recent passersby flashed before my eyes like a slideshow of my life. Fight or flight was not an option. It was my time to fight!

Imagining my family coming into my home to clean my brain off the wall pumped adrenaline through my body. Staring past Bone and fixated on the spot on the wall directly in front of me, but behind him, I could see me getting the gun from him, and his brains were plastered on the drywall. The image of this was clear to me. I had to picture that I was going to come out on top. It was no longer a second guess or wonder if I would make it out alive. His ass was good as dead. The very thought of it sent a surge of energy through my cells. The adrenaline rush was a quick shot to my kidneys, giving me a mental and physical boost. I needed that rush of strength to create space so I could kick him in his diaphragm. It was not working. His strength was overpowering me. He was an amateur boxer trained at the gym in Detroit. I tussled with guys on the streets and was an expert in ground fighting, thanks to the police academy. I brought my knees closer and pressed them into his waist, inching my way up; that is when *Angel* pushed up like she was pushing out a baby as hard as she could. All the while keeping an eye on his trigger finger. At this point I reconciled one of us was going to catch a bullet. But I would be damned if it were going to be me. *Angel* head-butted him. He lost control of the gun and fell off the bed. I had to move quickly. Hopping off the bed, *Angel* kicked the gun under the bed. He tried choking me. I could feel myself losing the battle against an enraged, jealous man. *Angel* examined the room for anything that could separate us. It was a waste of time and energy to pry his hands from around my neck. That's when the allegiance of *Angel* took total control. My beer mug was sitting on the nightstand next to the bed. As hard as she could, she smacked him over the head with the glass mug, and he dropped to his knees. He tried reaching for the gun. *Angel* kicked it further under the bed. By now my heart was pumping so hard, you could see it beating through my chest. I don't recall how *Angel* made it to the gun first, but she did! She dropped the clip, and while he was still on his knees, she stepped on his hand, crushing his fingers. To this day his finger is still bent from not getting it properly reset. She told him, "Assume the position." She wanted him to lie face down and put his hands behind his back. He refused to budge. "Assume the fucking position!" Bone thought I was going to cuff him and call the police.

The blood on my chin was dripping between my breasts. With each drip, the idea of a man whom I helped sort through his own life doing this to me sent me to another planet. Saturn, to be exact. My emotions were hotter than hell, and Angel was the devil in the flesh. I could hear him panting, like a dog that I thought he was at that moment. He remained in a kneeling position, out of breath. He would not assume the position. *Angel* gave Bone a helping hand. She kicked him in the back and reached for my cuffs on the nightstand. She warned him, "The gun is already racked with one in the chamber. I do not need that clip!" For good measure, she kicked him in the back of the head. He spread eagle, and *Angel* cuffed him. Weak from the fight he did not expect, Bone whimpered out, "Nikki, please do not execute me. I am sorry, I want us to talk." He could not think Nikki or *Angel* wanted to talk, with blood dripping from our mouths. "Shut up, punk. You sound like those bitches I get paid to deal with on those streets. Shut the fuck up!"

My emotions were raging. I was trying to suppress *Angel,* but *Angel* was winning. I laughed, I cried, I was mad. Nikki felt hurt. I defended his honor against my family, and now this. I yanked his pants off and placed the nose of the gun up to his ass. "If you so much as flinch, I'm going to pull this trigger, so help me God. If you make a sound, Imma pull it out and stick it in your mouth." He was shaking like he was having a seizure. "STOP MOVING BITCH! You were tough when you had this thing aimed at my head and down my throat!" Bone begged, "NIKKI NOOOOO PLEASE DON'T"! I ran the cold steel 9mm down his spine as if we were having foreplay, but Nikki was gone. *Angel* had completely taken over.

Nothing was going to stop *Angel* from torturing Bone. Nothing! She shoved the nozzle between the cheeks of his butt. Scared shitless that *Angel* was going to shove it in his hole, he began to groan. She could hear his internal cries. Fiercely irritated by the sound of his cry, *Angel* reminded Bone, "Nigha, you got friends who been to prison. You know how this shit goes. This shit ain't new to you." He tried to stifle his tears of agony as she twisted the gun in a circular motion. Teasing the idea of completely sodomizing him, just as promised, *Angel* yanked the gun from his tightly clenched cheeks and slid it across his lips. He tried to tighten his lips. He clenched his teeth so hard she could hear his jaw snap. "Now you know *Angel* can pry your mouth open, or you can just open it like a good boy." Scared, *Angel* was going to blow his head off. Bone sought the lesser evil option; he opened his mouth. Only because he opened his mouth *Angel* decided against putting it in his mouth. She laid the gun on the bed and reached for her work boots. Bone trembled in fear. He did not know what torture *Angel* was bringing next. She slowly laced her boots while sitting on the bed, looking down at Bone, and gave him a stern look. He struggled to press his face to the floor, attempting to avoid eye contact. *Angel* savagely said, "Pick your face up and have the same energy you had ten minutes ago." Bone sluggishly raised his head. Using Bone's back as a pedestal, *Angel* lifted herself off the bed. Walking beside him, she turned her back and gave him a donkey kick to the mouth. Bone calling the police was the last thing on my and *Angel's* mind.

#2

I called my partner, the one Bone was accusing me of. "Smitty, this Nikki, I need you to come to the house. Bone has something he wants to talk to you about. He wants a show." Anytime we mentioned a show, Smitty interpreted that meant we were about to do a Broadway performance. I could count on Smitty to help tidy up the mess. He was not much for words. He said, "Okay, give me ten." Thrilled to have Smitty join me, "Thanks, partner; you think I should make this a party and invite the bitch Bone screwing? Make it a two-for-one kind of night." That was my way of letting Bone know he was not as slick as he thought. His grease was too thin. I saw through it. I chose to ignore it. With his boyish chuckle, "Nahhh, I'll be there in ten." Bone looked like he was going into shock, so *Angel* poured freezing water on his face. "You bet' not die, punk. Stay alive so you can at least get the answer to your question." *Angel* hopped on the bed and waited for Smitty's arrival.

A brief time later, *Angel* could see Smitty's headlights. He pulled into the driveway. She laughed at Bone, taunting him for his inability to move, "Hey, I'm about to open the door for Sgt. Smitty, don't go nowhere." Given my history with Smitty, Bone discerned he was going to die a heinous death. Bone still trembling with fear and agony, "Nikki, why…let me leave. Don't you know…" Cutting Bone's sentence off with a hushing sound, finger to my lips, "shhhhhh", exiting through the bedroom door, *Angel* laughed, "Love huh, you love yo' momma, I bet she never had a pistol put down her throat."

23

Smitty was approaching the front door. *Angel* opened the door, "Welcome, partner, it's showtime!" The emphasis on showtime had Smitty cracking up with laughter. Angel led Smitty to her bedroom. In a soft pitch covering his mouth, "Nikki, what the hell is going on? I thought you told me everything was cool with y'all." The faintness of Smitty's voice brought me back to reality, "It was… until he knocked the piss out of me because he thinks we have been hooking up." With a surprised look and chuckle, Smitty exclaimed, "What, hooking up? Did you tell'em I am gay!" Nikki zealously responded, "Nope. Why should I… Now, look at what he made me do. All for naught."

Smitty's business was not mine to tell. Bluntly put, it was not Bone's business to know. Bone's jealousy was not that big of an issue for me. It was the idea that he believed that he could come in and make accusations, knowing full well he was out-sexing other women. The boldness of Bone to approach me about cheating. There is hardcore evidence he is sleeping with the white chick a few blocks around; I never questioned him about it. Things would have been so much easier if the guilt of what he was trying to do in my face was not consuming him. If he wanted to end things, he should have packed his things and left. No one was forcing him to stay. I was a convenience for him. I was a comfort. I was his meal ticket. Smitty listened to me rant, "Smit, do you believe the gumption of this clown! Out here sleeping with the enemy, using my money for a come-up, show him the ropes, now he wanna blow my head off because he thinks I'm screwing the pillow princess." Realizing I had gone too far by calling Smitty a *pillow princess*, I offered him an apology. Smitty began shaking his head, "Now you got to kill him."

#3

Smitty could not possibly believe I was going to kill him. Yeah, he could… but Bone…Killing Bone was not an alternative for me. *Angel* was going to finish him, but Nikki was back. "I am not going to kill him, Smitty. He is going to get up, shower, get his things and do not look back." By the look on Smitty's face, he was not agreeable to letting him go alive. "You trust this sucker won't talk." Picking up the glass

24

pieces and remnants of evidence, I turned to Smitty, "I'm pretty sure he's not going to tell anyone he was violated with a gun by his girl." Smitty and I continued to clean and step around Bone while he lay there listlessly, cuffed on the floor. I pulled him up and sat him against the wall.

I was disgusted by what happened but mortified by the audacity of Bone to confront me like that, knowing I had his best interest. I do not take betrayals lightly. I spoke to him gently, "Bone, when we finish cleaning up the mess you started, you are going to get showered. Go your way, and I will go mine. Smitty will take you to the airport, and when you land wherever you want to go, I will have your things shipped to you. FYI, as you heard, Smitty is gay, and it was the trick baby you are fucking with who dropped the dime on you to your employers. She was big mad because you would not leave me for her. My people kept a hawk's eye on her. I keep an eye on the sky, ears on the streets, and boots on the ground. Let me remind Bone, who is dealing with this, "Next time, handle your scandal better, my friend!" Having an assembly of connections was beneficial for me. A lot of cases were closed because of my contacts, police and personal cases.

Smitty took Bone to the airport for me. I could trust Smitty to do just that, even though I know he wants Bone dead. Smitty and I have worked together most of our careers on the force. He became a sergeant. Some people want the title. I don't want the hassle of dealing with too many people and their personalities. Dealing with my own personality was a handful. Being an investigator was good enough for me. Besides, I do too much side work to add anything else to my plate.

I cleaned myself up and tried to decompress. A myriad of thoughts ran through my mind. I could not believe *Angel* would show up and show out. Consequently, Bone introduced himself to *Angel*. Why God? Why? After all that Bone put me through on Angel's Night, I still had to work the beat the next day. The same way, I must go in tomorrow and nosy around the *Mr. Magic* case. It was no surprise to me that Bone resurfaced two years later, bringing me a bone. I could have shot him in the leg on Angel's Night that year, and he would still look out for me. That is the kind of bond we have. He realized he had crossed me the wrong way, and this was his way of redeeming himself.

7

DIGITAL MAGIC

Lieutenant Chapman was the first face to greet me inside the precinct. Chap was a big man in stature. His attitude was just as big. Nobody at the job or on the streets messes around with him. He was not an angry man but a man about business. Police business was his priority, and everyone around him knew it. He had a hard-on for shady officers. That is why I tip-toed around him to get the intel I needed for the Magic case.

"Hey Chap, what you know good?" In typical Lieutenant Chapman fashion, Chap shrugged his shoulders and said, "I know you need to keep a better eye on your colleagues; Smitty called in today. It is his second call off this week." Smitty did not mention anything going on in his personal life. Not anything alarming enough to warrant me calling him. Respectfully, "I'll give him a call when I make my sick and shut-in rounds, Lieu." I blew right past Chap before he could get another word out. Smitty has called in quite a bit. He takes care of himself. Not assuming the worst. I am not one for assuming just because he is homosexual every time he calls off, it must be the three-letter package. Lt. Chapman on the other hand, is thinking that. He jumps straight to worse-case scenarios, only for the opposite to transpire. My bet is Smitty ran off somewhere to get married. Smitty met a handsome man online, and they were hanging out quite a bit. I think they complement each other well. However, what Smitty does in his world is on him. I can't focus on him right now because my world is so jacked up right now.

I need to tighten up the two reports parked in my queue. I also have an interview with an informant on a human trafficking case. Hangtown was remarkably close to Detroit. There was an uptick in crime in the area. The streets of Hangtown were becoming a hot spot for heroin addicts and prostitution. One bad decision is ruining these children's lives. The victims are getting younger and younger in the human trafficking cases. If I could unleash *Angel* on all the saps that took advantage of people when they were at their weakest, I would! No wonder so many officers suffer from alcoholism and substance abuse themselves. Xanax became my best friend after that saga with Bone. I was managing well. Talking to a therapist would land both of us in prison. So, I leaned on the Xannies. I was able to cope with the things I experienced and witnessed on the job. The first time I killed a civilian sent me into shock, but it was justifiable. It was the work outside of work that kept me popping Xanax and sipping wine. I traded in my two packs of smokes and cognac after a health scare.

The ancestors of Hangtown are probably flipping in their graves. Hangtown used to be an affluent area with beautiful brick bungalows and ranch-style houses. Most of the residents were entrepreneurs, but since a lot of the older generation passed away, the houses were being rented out by various investors, mostly Airbnb. I chose to stay, at least close by. I had hope for Hangtown.

I checked the CRISNET database for the sergeant's approval of the reports I drafted yesterday. I also checked to see if the Magic case had updates and detectives' notes. So far there was nothing that stood out. CRISNET showed Magic's case as a missing persons case. A bag of tools, *no pun intended*, of potential witnesses was included in the report. Only a third of potential witnesses and suspects were interviewed. That was my gateway to see if the lead investigator could use my assistance. That would be the perfect opening to get next to witnesses and see exactly what Bone was talking about. It was less polluted to deal directly with witnesses than to keep snooping in the recorded database. The database records an officer's logins, the record officer's profile, the date, time, and even how long each page was open. Policing the police. There is always more than one way to skin a cat!

I made sure not to study the report too long. I walked over to the lead investigator, Officer Shagwell. Shagwell was always testy. He drank energy drinks. Those things gave him more than energy. His energy level was that of a toddler at the theme park. A cocky son of a biscuit. I will have to butter his biscuit if I want to get gravy on the Magic case. "Hey, Shagwell, you look like you just came from the gym. How is everything going…with your lady and the new pooch?" Shagwell could tell I was up to something. It is not like he is ignorant of the fact that I had a relationship with Magic. Snarkily, "Harris, everyone and everything is fine. What can I do for you?" Since you asked, "It's not what you can do for me, but what I can do for you." Before I told him what it was, "No Harris, NO to whatever it is!" Returning the same energy but adding a little sugar on top, "Yes, Shagwell, YES, you have a crap load of witnesses to interview, and you have not touched a quarter of them. You need some help. Look, I know Magic, and I had a thing, and it would be unethical to have me on the case, but I want to know what happened to him, too. I have mad love for the man. If something happened to your girl, wouldn't you want to know…in fact, do not answer that because I know you would want to know. You would flip the earth over finding out." I wanted to remind him about all the times he had me looking into his side piece's boyfriends. He wanted me to do an illegal stop on her main guy. I did it because that was our unspoken, unethical code of loyalty. Deliberately turning my back to him and propping my butt on his desk, I sipped hot cocoa and then waited for him to fold. Shagwell was smart enough to read the room. There was no mention of the favors he called in. He could read what I was saying without me saying it. "Alright, Harris, look, this is huge. Come on, the guy is well-known. He may have dibbled and dabbled into illegal betting, but for the most part, his past is clean. You know I can't give you ala carte access to the case. You will get a heads up if anything comes out." Graciously, I thanked Shagwell, "Thanks, Bro, that's all your lil' sis wants."

Hot footing it back to my desk, thinking about the nerve of Shagwell, "*A heads up*". Heads up is cryptic for you'll find out when we come knocking at your door. My goal is to get a jump on things, Magic disappearing into thin air was truly a mystery. Is it possible that I blanked out, and Angel went ballistic? Hiding evidence, sure, that is what I do, but bodies. No way! Since Shagwell was going to play it by the book, there was no need to bug him about it. There was still my assigned work to finish. Stretching and sighing, I was not ready to hop on my cases. Maleeky Richard was at the forefront of my things to do.

8

AROMA MAGIC

Whenever I hopped in the scout car with Detective Hollis, I wanted to holler. This officer was so rank his odor permeated through the vehicle. He smelt like a rotten potato wrapped in old bologna. Hollis was a sweetheart, though. We confidentially talked about our personal lives quite a bit. Our conversations reminded me of my talks with my sisters. At least I knew Hollis and I shared secrets that never ran through the rumor mill of the department. I was not so sure if I could give him all the tea on me and Magic. I could inquire about his knowledge of the case without raising flags. It would not be the first time I used him as my source of internal intel. I could ask him anything, and it would not raise those furry, overgrown eyebrows on his face, "Hey Hollis, what is the word on Magic? Any juicy intel?" Not expecting the rotten potato to go deeper than my line of question, but he did! "If my darling Nikki did not do it, then my darling Nikki would have nothing to worry her darling head about. Besides, how did you get yourself entangled with a guy like Magic?" Hollis' inquisition into my line of questions made me feel like I needed to invoke Garrity Rights. Garrity Rights is a form of protection for public employees against self-incrimination during an investigatory interview, usually done by Internal Affairs.

9

A RABBIT OUT THE HAT

Hollis' voice gave off an uncle who is a police officer vibe. The *you know you fucked up now* voice. It could be intimidating at times, but our rapport gave me a sense of contentment when sharing with him. For this topic, I proceeded with caution. When you jump in the car with Hollis, you never know what the day brings. He needs to bring me the inside scoop on Magic so I can start planning. I was going to plan my defense or plan my getaway. Nonetheless, cruising the streets of Hangtown with Hollis is always colorful.

I tried to ignore his question. When we passed by Magic's office on Fort Street, I felt compelled to answer him. "Believe it or not, he magically appeared in my D.M. app." He turned his head to face the driver's side window and shockingly asked, "What's a D.M.?" Hollis' old self was not social media savvy. He was old, but not so old he could not keep up with the police work. Telling him about my encounter with Magic is going to be challenging. Especially with explaining any technical details. "D.M.-Direct Messenger, it's another channel of communication." His expression told me he wanted a more detailed account other than our initial encounter.

There was only so much I could share. The case is still open, and the streets are still talking. Magic may have been a show, but I was a small part of that show. He had the lead role in my drama. I thought I fell in love with Magic. I often questioned whether I loved him or the potential in him. Just like Bone and I, Magic and I shared things in common. We both worked our way up the ladder. I had more education than Magic, but he was good at what he did. He was an intellectual. It was a mental stimulation when I was with him. Not always physical. Magic was an eclectic individual. He thought of himself as a complex individual with layers. I thought of him as a chameleon, adapting to whatever environment he was in. Magic could hold a conversation with anyone, no matter their rank or title. He was a well-rounded, blue-collar guy. He had knowledge of everything from his handy man trade to stocks and bonds.

His thoughts flowed deeply, but his heart was shallow. He was seventeen years my senior and extremely tall in stature, standing six feet nine. Older men were not my thing. Maleeky had a youthfulness about himself. He moved with the grace of a swan, not in a feminine way, but in a way that he was light on his feet. That was unusual for a man his height. No clumsiness, no slouching, his walk was prideful, shoulders back with his nose in the air. His style was leisure. He wore gym shoes with ankle socks and tracksuits all year round, and he loved exposing his freckled fair complexion in the sun. The sun kissed his skin, giving him a golden glow. Magic looks like he could be the biological father to New York Yankee's right fielder, Aaron Judge. The resemblance is uncanny. His body was ripped with muscles; he had a baseball player's physique with an eagle's wingspan. Looking at him sent chills down my spine in a good way.

Talking about Magic struck a chord. For one, people were thinking I had something to do with his disappearance, although not named a suspect yet. Also, he fleetingly held a special place in my heart. My trust issues were so bad that me to give anyone a shot at wooing my heart was a huge leap. I dated around and married once, but none captivated my heart the way Magic did. Truth is, I did not know if I would ever see him again, dead or alive. After our last night together, I am pretty sure he did not want to see me alive if he was somewhere alive.

I snapped out of my reminiscing to answer Hollis, "What Magic and I shared was sacred. You could consider it mystical. Magic taught me a lot, including how to lay a ceramic floor. Magic was a genius in his own rite. He made himself too accessible, and that is why it is hard to pin the details of his disappearance (awkward silence) …In which I had nothing to do with." I thought adding the disclaimer would abate any suspicion of me. At least it would for Nikki. I was a little apprehensive about what *Angel* may have done. Trying to make Hollis laugh, I compared my romantic situationship with Magic to Richard Gere and Julia Robers in the movie *Pretty Woman*. Realistically, that's how I started to feel, like I was his hired help, and he was my older John.

#2

Welp, this was our stop. We arrived at the Liquor Store on Concord and Jefferson Ave. Someone spotted the subject in a human trafficking case sitting in a white van while he sent a worker bee into the store. They called the tipline. The warrant was issued months ago. He was known on the streets as Ant, short for Anthony. These young guys think they are invincible. They left more breadcrumbs on the streets than Magic left at my doorstep. It was not hard to find them.

Out of all the crimes to commit, this is the one that puzzled me on so many levels. The men were opportunists. They would catch women in their vulnerable state and reel them in. What if it were their mothers, sisters, aunts? Do not get me wrong, there are men being trafficked too. There were no boundaries in sex crimes. It affects everyone.

Arresting Ant had me increasingly thinking about my relationship with Magic. If you could ever really title it a relationship. We related to each other but in a deeply superficial way. I realized the way he made me feel, is how he made everyone he engaged with feel. His romantic aura radiated a magical eminence. He was self-aware and used his gifts to work his magic. I thought about how Maleeky roped me in. It was during a time when I let my guard down and wanted to feel appreciated and loved. I no longer wanted to be the strong Black woman who could manage any situation, but I wanted the comfort of a gentleman. A man who could be considerate of my emotions, my feelings, and my finances. I was eager to display my soft feminine side. My exterior was tough, but my heart longed for an empathetic man, a compassionate man, one who would respect my work in the police department and the ability to make good things happen on the home front.

The men around the department talk about their wives and significant others, wanting to collect an allowance for their hard-earned work. I was not that woman. After trying to be supportive of the two men I cared most for and experiencing their perfidy, I no longer could see myself being that emotionally and financially supportive woman ever again. It scared me to think that *Angel* would resurrect and infinitely walk the face of the earth.

#3

Hollis and I finished the report and took Ant to the holding cell. Ant was familiar with me. I locked him up before. As usual, he wanted me to know he would not stay behind bars long, "Officer Harris…Nikki? Right? I will see you again…Soon. Be safe out there; you do not want to be the one responsible for stopping money from circulating in the hood." If Ant knew my brother-in-law, he would stick a sock in his own mouth. Both brothers-in-law, Rod and Keith, are highly influential and tied to business and the streets. Keith also had backing from the church. Nothing about Ant was menacing to me. Truth be told, he was the kind that I would handle myself. No *Angel* needed. Prosecutors had a hard time convicting him. His victims would not show up to court, and some were coached into believing they really wanted a life of drugs and prostitution from state to state. Hopefully, the Feds will nab him, and it will stick.

Rod Crapanzano, an Italian man, Wendy's, husband; is a businessperson who controlled the majority of businesses in Florida and the Detroit communities because he heavily invested in them. His money ran the streets. He may even use Magic's work to restore vacant houses he invests in. We did not discuss business with him. When I vacationed to see them, it was strictly about family and fun. Not a living soul was brazened enough to ask Rod about his business. You cannot ask Rod his real name. He uses Rod, but his first name is feminine in Western culture, so he goes by something more masculine. To this day, that information remains sealed. It was sealed to the outside world, but of course, I know "Rod's" government name is Camille Crapanzano. However, Rod was audacious enough to ask about my personal life.

We wrapped things up with Ant and hopped back into the car, where I took the passenger side. There was plenty to think about. The memory of Rod asking me about who I was bringing to his Annual Entrepreneurial Recognition Gala festered in my thoughts. "Nikki, who will be the pick of the season this year?" When I mentioned the name Magic, Rod froze in place. His reaction to my response suspended my question: *what is the problem?* I kept it to myself. Apprehension kept me from pressing for any scoop Rod could offer me about my newfound love. At that point, Rod did not know how deep my feelings for Magic were. The rabbit was out of the hat. Now, the whole family would know "Nikki" is fooling around with Mr. Magic.

Jarring myself from thinking about my history with Magic, I pulled out my personal cell phone and scrolled through TikTok while Hollis drove us back to the precinct. The photographic images in my phone of Magic and me broke my concentration. They popped up as a memory in the picture gallery. It was a picture of us horseback riding. We had that in common. Picture after picture popped up. Looking at all our photos, someone might think we've been together longer than we have. Shortly after we met, we took a vacation to Maldives. It was already on his list of things to do, and he invited me to join him. It was obvious this was not his first time. The theme at Magic Island had a Maldives vibe to it. We stayed in a private villa with our own private lakefront beach. My first impression was not bad for a handyman's special. His investments must have afforded him the more luxurious things. He was not prudent with his money, often spent on frivolities. Somehow, he managed to squeeze in multiple vacations in less than a year's time.

10

STAGE MAGIC

A little less than a year of being away from Bone, Magic invited me to his home for rest and relaxation. "Come to the Island. I would like to get to know you." It was the summer of 2017. I was skeptical about joining him. I was not ready. I had divorced once and practically killed Bone's clown ass for smacking me. I could not risk another man tickling my fancy only to betray me. Being alone did not bother me much. It was attaching myself to people who deceived me when what I asked for was a very small facet in the grand scheme of it all. Considering giving my heart was a big piece of me, why should I give my heart when being honest is an arduous task for humans.

My first visit with Magic was unparallel to anything I had experienced. He called his estate Magic Island. The waterfront residence was overflowing with beauty. The marshy grounds bestow a serene, majestic and mystical beauty. He had four acres of splendor. The grounds were immaculate. It looked like artificial grass and a freshly paved blacktop driveway with iron gates surrounding the land. A makeshift pond with goldfish spans in a half-moon around the back perimeter of the land. You had to have the PIN to enter the gate. The soft, aromatic fragrance of lilacs and lilies infused the air. It has a wow factor! Mother nature's touch on the property was nothing short of perfection; right in Hangtown City. Magic presented me with a soft, gentle side that I yearned for. Before he reached for my hand, he asked if it was okay to touch me. I was comfortable with his touch. Moreso captivated by his looks and admiration for beauty. He grabbed me by the hand and led me towards the back of his dwellings. To be a laborer, he had soft and manicured hands. I spotted a motorcycle parked outside of the detached garage. To look at him, you would never think he was into motorcycles. I had him pegged to be a sports car enthusiast. That was something we did not have in common. There was a garage attached to the house, and the detached brick storage space was for his motorcycle collection.

As beautiful and serene as Magic Island was, something was off. My instinct has never failed me. At times, I could feel when something was going to happen instantly. Then, there were times when the feeling of a premonition came over me. I felt weirded out. To get to the bottom of my suspicions, I had to start with the origin of his name, *Maleeky Richard*. Whose mother names them Maleeky? Obviously, his mother did, but she had to know Dick is the short version of Richard. Asking him about how the name came about was fair for a first encounter. With a childish giggle, but seriously wanting to know, "Maleeky, where did that name come from?" Magic looked me in the eyes, "I see my little grasshopper wants a history lesson…Maleeky is the extended version of Maleek. My mother, who is half Arabic and African American, named me Maleek, which means 'owner'. The 'y' was added to distinguish me from my father, Maleek Richard. She did not want me to be classified as a junior because of his lack of presence in my life." We shared that in common. He was over fifty years old, and I wondered if his father's absence affected him the same way it affected me, not having my own. Something in his voice told me if it does the signs will manifest eventually. Maybe that was the eeriness I was feeling. We were more of a twin flame.

My attention shifted to the handy work done to the house, which did not look like a professional did it. No need to ask who did the work because Maleeky Richard was proud to boast of all the updates he did to his home. He claimed it was all done as a one-man job, with no help from anyone. I resisted the urge to state my opinion, that it shows no help was contracted.

Surprisingly, Magic resided in Hangtown. It is on the beaten path of Detroit neighborhoods. A bustling city, but I thought he would prefer a more secluded home. His house had all the bells and whistles, but it was not a gated community or subdivision. When he invited me to Magic Island, I envisioned a majestic castle.

Nevertheless, his presence excited me. He exuded a regal ambiance. Magic wanted to take a motorcycle ride. Speaking to me the way an instructor speaks to their student, "Nikki, one of the best ways to relax your mind is to peruse the scenery and assess what others are doing. It is the only way to get to know your community and network with those around you. You get a chance to take time to smell the roses you trample over when you are out there chasing criminals." A subtle way for him to show me his humorous side. Magic must assume I am a beat cop. I was past my prime for chasing criminals. Here nor there, he had me geeked to ride his Harley.

A forewarning would have been nice especially since we were going through the murky terrains of Hangtown. My selection of a sundress would have stayed in the drawer. Magic offered to get me a change of clothes, "Nikki, would you like to put on a pair of my jeans and shirt?" "Thanks, but no thanks, Magic. Your pants might fit like capris." Magic was impressed with my sarcasm. His pants legs would drag the ground on me…and I got height. We are both tall, but no way could I fit a man's pair of jeans. Riding on a Harley in a sundress! First time for everything.

Strangely, I was comfortable hanging out with Magic. I was letting my guard down and ignoring my intuition. One of my fellow officers lived nearby. I sent Officer Jamison a text to let her know I was in the area. This was a customary practice for Jamison and me. We did not go anywhere without letting someone know who we were with and what we were doing. In the event something happened, at least one other officer would have an insight into the last known location and people we were hard knobbing with. Besides, Jamison was my backup pair of eyes.

Magic suggested we head back to his home after riding on the Harley. I was glad about it. Our mini tour of Detroit was exhausting and exhilarating in the same breath. Trying to keep my dress from flying over my face. Things were going so well; it spooked me. Magic has a reputation that supersedes him. A clever businessperson who loved making cocktails and having touchy feelies. We did not drink any alcoholic beverages. Therefore, breaking his wrist was not at the forefront of my thoughts. Food was preoccupying my thoughts. All the wind I took in from not wearing a helmet had my empty stomach rumbling.

I worked up my appetite. Magic wanted to get the grill going and the drinks stirring. Welp, not drinking alcoholic beverages, was brief. Magic offered me a cocktail. He wanted me to make it for myself as well, "Nikki, you are more than welcome to fix yourself a drink. I have all the ingredients on my bar, there's a Blender sitting on the top of the ice machine next to the bar." I had the feeling Magic wanted me to make my own drink to make me feel comfortable that he was not slipping me any foreign substances to inhibit my judgment. Thinking about his touchy-feely reputation I declined, "Thanks, Magic, maybe some other time, I will have some cucumber, lemon water and dress it like a cocktail." He had more than chicken breast planned on his menu. He wanted a taste of Nikki! "After we eat, I have a surprise for you." Tenderly gazing into his eyes, I wondered what kind of surprise. It was my first visit there. Coughing, to mask my reluctance, "A surprise. I am not up for surprises. Can we eat and talk a little bit, get to know each other better." His glasses slid down the bridge of his nose, and his eyes peered over the top of the black frames he wore. He strutted away, walking towards the grille in disbelief that someone declined his gesture of spontaneity. This enthused me. It was clear our personalities rejected the word *no*. I called him by his government name, "Maleeky, I appreciate everything you have done today, but I only set aside a little time to spend with you. If it is okay, you can surprise me tomorrow." Magic did not waste any time, "Sure sweetheart, duly note Maleeky is a busy man, there's money to be made. I do not chase pussy. I attract money." He winked at me with a fervor that almost made me change my mind. "Ok, Magic, let's eat so I can go and get ready for work."

As distasteful as I found his comment, I understood what he meant. A. If he was dealing with a person, he was looking for an opportunity to make money or B. If he was romantically interested, he was not going to waste time getting to the good part. He wanted what he wanted when he wanted it. From the sounds of it, he was more interested in money than relationships. No rush to return to work, but someone had to do it. Retention in the department was dwindling. It was hard to recruit fresh talent. Being an officer used to be prestigious, but not so much since school attendance was dropping and the youth were being exposed to promising six-figure salaries. It was more buzzing around being an entrepreneur than being an officer or firefighter. Teachers were suffering a shortage as well.

11

LEVITATION

Hollis and I made our way back to the station. "Uncle Hollis" had a way with words, "Time to suck it up, buttercup." There was chaos from the parking lot to the inside of the precinct. Our jurisdiction is not as big as Detroit's. There were only three precincts. Scout cars were racing out of the precinct parking lot. We did not hear anything come over the radio. I asked Hollis if he thought we should see if dispatch had dispatched all scouts, and we somehow missed it! That would totally suck, but I liked Hollis' idea better, "We are here now, let's just go in and see what all the commotion is about." We used the front entrance instead of the usual back entrance. This way, we could talk to station security and the desk officers. They should have knowledge of what was going on. They did! The Lieutenant was the first person I saw. "Lt. Chap, what's going on? Do they need us out there?" Lt. Chapman, dragging his baritone voice, adjusting his utility belt, "No Nikki, looks like they found a uhhh, a uhhh... close to Clinton Twp." Of course, I had to ask why our investigators were blaring out of the lot for an "uhhhh" in Clinton Twp. My gut boiling over with the Mexican food Hollis and I ate, mixed with anxiety about Magic's whereabouts, my head started pounding because I knew it was all over for me. My career went down the toilet, and my chance to start a family was ruined. The atmosphere in the precinct told me this was about Magic.

Hollis summoned me to come closer to him. He was talking with one of the desk officers. They always have tea to spill. The desk officers were usually disabled and sat there to take reports from incoming citizens. They were privy to the happenings from the inside out. In what was supposed to be a whisper, Hollis, with an empathetic voice,

42

"Nikki, it is Magic. They are saying it is Magic. They found Mr. Magic's body." My eyes rolled to the back of my head. Blood rushed to my temples. My gut flipped inside out. I tried to keep my composure, but I found it difficult to maintain. Thoughts were running through my head as if they were an Olympic track star. Was he in the water? Woods? Why the hell was he in Clinton Township? How did he get there? It wasn't me. Is he clothed? Was his dog Teddy nearby? Are there any items linking me to him? What if his spooky ass somewhere levitating off the ground? Nowhere to turn and no one to talk to. The point of no return. This was going downhill and fast. I wanted to be there. I wanted to see him. I needed to see him; this could not be true. My thoughts, *ANGEL, WHAT DID YOU DO*? I yelled it on the inside of my mind, slowly turning away from Hollis. Hollis was good at reading me. I had to walk away. He would detect I knew more than I lead on to. His intuition was stronger than mine. His wisdom and knowledge from being on the force longer gave him a third eye. He could see straight through me. It was best for me to just walk away.

In a concentrated walk back to Lt. Chap, my immediate exchange was, "Lieu, I'm going to need a few days off to process this. As you know, Magic and I were good friends." Oh shit, I said, we 'were' instead of we are…The lieutenant will take note of the tense and assume I know more than what I let on to know. The asshole could not wait to say, "Officer Harris, you will need more than a few days. You are going on Administrative Leave and turning in your service gun until you get Internal Affairs a statement of your last interactions with Maleeky Richard, aka Mr. Magic…Dick, my gosh, you people have more names than the roll call roster. Hopefully, this will be all sorted out, and we will not have to process you." Did he just say *you people*? I was not worried about the consequences. I was worried about the comment Lieutenant Chapman made. That was the reason Hangtown was called Hangtown. There was a history of subliminal bias in the city. Seriously, they had to follow standing operating procedures, and there were people they had to go through before they could name me a suspect. First, they had to confirm the body was indeed Magic's. My union steward will hear from me soon. The union president will have to put my dues to good use.

12

CONTROL

Through the chaos and mayhem, finally, I made it to the locker room. I collected my thoughts. The shift had not ended. No qualms about any officers pussyfooting around here. My first thought was to not panic. Thinking to myself, *keep your composure. Stay in control, Nikki. Keep Angel under control. Don't lash out at anyone.* Yet, I was panicking. Did they find his body? Was he dismembered? Did they find his ponytail? I remember thinking about cutting the silky strands, but I don't recall either of us doing it. I need more details. I will not write a statement until there are more details. Even if my superiors connected any dots, there was never any intention of allowing them to control the narrative. A mental note was made well before this day came. Anytime *Angel* crosses the line, I rehearse the defense. I will give Lieutenant my gun and make my way home. I cannot call Celeste and Wen just yet. Celeste's voice was branded in my brain. I could hear her now. *See, I told you, you going to end up on the other side of the law. What the hell you out there doing, Nikki? I can't save you from this. Only God can do it, Nikki.* Wendy would step in to intervene before Celeste, and I got into a full-fledged blowout. *Celeste, hush, what is done is done. We must let things play out and see where this goes, or should I say where Nikki is going.* Both of their voices would be a nuisance in my ear right now. Although they both would have valid assessments. I need to see evidence before making a decision. Sure enough, I need God right now! I will give Rod a call. Rod was resourceful. I will call Jamison for sure. I must find out if she heard or saw anything the last night I was with Maleeky. At this point, trusting anyone is nil.

I wondered if Bone knew they found a body. Usually, he would contact me at the first mention of something on local news or social media. Where is he? Bone had no issues calling to tell me the streets were talking. He should be on my phone now arranging a furtive meeting. I emphatically do not want Bone to be anywhere near my house. They will have eyes on my house until they can swoop in and hang me on the hook for this. I do not want them to implicate Bone for anything. I do not want investigators to interview or interrogate Bone. He might slip up to tell them something about Angel's Night. I was deeply disappointed with Bone, but I did not want anything to happen to him. Bone and I called a truce. We knew we could not be together as a couple. We would always look out for each other. It has been my observation that the strongest, toughest guys will sing like a canary to keep from doing a bit. They even take pleas to crimes they did not commit, all to avoid doing long prison sentences. My thoughts are all over the place. The locker room smelled of shampoo and spritz. I needed to get out of there. Moments like this had a nostalgic feel in Hangtown. The era my grandmother talked about. They were going to pin this on me whether I did it or not. Deep down, I knew I was somewhat responsible, but I could not erase the fact, I left Magic in Magic Island alive. Not well, but alive. Hoping the body was not his and he was somewhere at the private villa in the Maldives, my mouth uttered the words without sound, *'Magic, come home, let's figure this out.'*

I am going home to get rest. Things were taking a toll on me.

13

PREDICTION

As bad as I wanted to call Celeste and Wendy, even my mother-Terry, I just could not bring myself to do it. Once I made it through my side door, I went straight to my room. I used the side door because it was closest to my detached garage. If this made it to the news, my neighbors would gawk and talk. Really, it is not about if it makes it to the news; it is when it makes it to the news. Magic was popular and either you loved him, or you hated him. At some point, I genuinely loved him. I loved being with him. Magic was wrestling with his own demons.

I stood in the room, right in the spot where *Angel* got Bone together. Then my body dropped to the bed. I mustered the energy to remove my clothes. Removing my clothes sent me down memory lane. I recall one conversation Magic, and I had when we first started messing around. "Maleeky, what happens if you do not recover Mr. Magic's Restoration business? What will you do? The more you borrow, the more indebted you become." In a flat, nonchalant manner, "I will go down with it. I will bury myself alive before I see that happen." The thought that Magic did this to himself moved into my frontal lobe. He was not getting the business he was used to. Times were changing. He was robbing Peter to pay Paul. Somehow, he mysteriously stayed afloat. He was managing all his extracurricular activities and living life to the fullest. That is how it appeared. My guess is Magic was into more than what he led on to be, and he had to get away. He used the opportunity of what transpired between us to make a great escape.

Trying to convince a jury that my last encounter with Maleeky, he was still alive, is going to be daunting. I mean, I have been on again and off again with Magic for a little over a year and a half. During that time, I cannot count the number of people that disconnected themselves from him, for one reason or another. He never took accountability for his indiscretions. Although, he had the charisma and charm to reel anyone in. Most discovered behind the mask is a Christmas turkey filled with shit!

Magic would brag that his dick saw more pussy than a toilet seat. As if it was a badge of honor to run through women. He was afraid of commitment. We never discussed what made him choose the lifestyle he flaunted. The only thing that came to mind was him being raised by a single woman. He did not mention his mother much at all. The things we discussed were the present and future. He steered away from his childhood and past.

When it came to the women in Magic's life, he unfamiliarized himself with closing the door, literally and figuratively. If it were some sort of game, he would introduce the women he was wooing to each other. The introduction would come in a face-to-face get-together or through pictures he sent to your cell phone. According to Magic, everyone was beautiful or talented in some way. He wanted the world to know he knew people, and people knew him. At times, I thought he had a genuine love for people; that was his way of sharing his circle with the ones he loved. Then, it became obvious this was his way of triangulation. A narcissistic ploy to have women competing for his affection. There were at least three women who came to my mind as potential suspects. Angel, Sheila, and Leidy.

#2

TURNING WINE INTO WISDOM

Magic loved to have guests over for dinner. This is where I met Sheila. Sheila's energy was revealing. It gave me more insight into the man, Maleeky. He introduced me as his friend and told me Sheila happened to stop by while she was in the neighborhood. I could tell Sheila was not overjoyed by my presence. Which let me know there was something more between the two of them. Instantly, my feeling about her was that of an old romantic partner. Her aura told the whole story. She was not a happenstance. They had a deep affiliation with each other. While offering to pour her a glass of wine, she dismissed my offer. *Did Sheila reject my offer of wine?* No offense was taken. She probably did not drink, which was my inclination. She probably didn't trust me to pour her a drink. We engaged in small talk about our careers and other idle topics. Sheila disclosed she is a retired registered nurse. She might be a health-conscious freak, which explains her decline to any spirits. Strangers never get much information about my personal life from me. Chances are I already know more about them than they do me. My focus shifted to the other guests in attendance. My ears caught Sheila throwing potshots at Magic. I attempted to excuse myself from the picnic table. Sheila abruptly began to quiz me, "Are you enjoying your visit to Magic Island? Be careful!" WOW! Keeping my cool because I did not know where the night was going, I tried to keep it short and sweet, "Well, Ms. Sheila, as a matter of fact, I am. Hope you join us more often!" This was a messy introduction. I hope she did not think she was intimidating me. I do not get frightened easily. Not knowing if this was going any further, removing my glasses, my eyes focused on the wine bottle. In case I must assist Sheila with snapping out of whatever she was going through. She did not appear to be a violent woman. Unless there is a call for duty, I would not consider myself a violent one either. Now *Angel,* on the other hand, will get things in order. *Dear God, please don't let me have to introduce Magic's guests to Angel.*

I continued to excuse myself from the table to go inside. Magic's dog, Teddy, greeted me with puppy kisses. Sheila came in shortly after me. She must have wanted to talk in private. I learned early on how to pick a person's brain. I asked closed-end questions or made off-kilter comments. Either way, I will get what I am looking for. I told Sheila where the bathroom was and to walk past Teddy. He was friendly. Sheila rolled her eyes and gave a fully loaded potato response, "Yeah, Teddy is friendly with everyone Maleeky let's in his house." Her prim demeaner was hotter than a potato, too. It told me all I needed to know. She was remarkably familiar with Maleeky and Teddy and with the floorplan of the house. I waited in the Florida room while Sheila used the bathroom. Disappointment was an understatement regarding how I was feeling. Sheila returned outside, and I stayed inside. Outside of me leaving the premises, it was the most reasonable option. I was not going to leave because I was an invited guest. I most certainly intended on having a word with Magic.

He had cameras and intercoms all over the house. I glared through the dining room window, which gave a perfect view of the two of them standing at the side door of the bungalow, just below the cameras. I turned on the intercom and listened to Sheila tell Maleeky, "Get your shit together, Maleeky, you owe me!" She stormed through the gates and drove off. I quickly flicked off the intercom and stepped away from the window. Pretending to clean the kitchen from all the food we made, I waited for Magic to return inside. Magic waited for at least another twenty minutes to come through the door. He looked like Puff the Magic Dragon, standing there puffing on his tobacco pipe.

14

WAVING THE WAND

Maleeky was so discombobulated that his peacock strut turned to a staggering gait. It looked like he had too much to drink, or Sheila gave him an *Angel*-style smack across the face. He stumbled through the kitchen, nearly stepping on Teddy. "Magic, we need to talk, but I'll wait for you to relax." Magic mumbled his words, "What's there to talk about, Nikki? Sheila is my friend and business partner. She is a recovering alcoholic. I should have mentioned that before you offered up some wine. She has been going through a divorce with her gay husband. What else do you need to know?" Before he could make it to the bedroom and crash out, I stopped him in his tracks, "An old friend, pfffttt. Naaahhhh brother…I do not think so, and maybe her husband is detecting the same 'more than friends' tension I feel between the two of you. Wait until you sleep it off and come up with something better than that." Whenever Magic did not want to discuss something, he had a way of deflecting. He would try to ward off my "Q & A" session to something about business or sex. Usually, there was not an in-between. "Come to bed, Nikki, let's get some sleep. I'll get the dishes in the morning." That was typical of him. Evading questions. If there was a dollar donated to my pockets every time he evaded questions, I would be a rich woman.

I wanted to leave, but I wanted face-to-face answers. Not only that but after months of unprotected sex, I needed to reaffirm I was the only one he was sexing. I fell in love with a scoundrel. Something I had never felt before. Lying next to Magic on my side of his California king-size bed, I started to rationalize the events. He may as well have waved a magic wand. Once he wrapped his arms around me and drifted into a deep sleep, I was even more smitten. Smitten by the fact

I was waking up next to Magic. His breath, with a hint of lemon and ginger, had an aphrodisiac quality that was intoxicating me. The incident between Magic and Sheila had no effect on the way I felt by his touch, the feeling of security he offered me. I chalked things up to Sheila being a bitter old bitty. She may have been seeking comfort from a friend slash business partner while divorcing. The story was relatable. When I went through my divorce, I leaned on Bone, but we admittedly went from text to sex. Besides, Magic always said *he did not want anything old but gold.* Sheila was older than me. I later discovered Sheila was worth more than gold to Magic.

15

PRODUCTION

My brain was on fire. I struggled to remember pertinent details of my last night with Magic. Certain it was sometime in September because the weather was not too hot or too cold. Then again, in Michigan, you cannot judge the time of the year by the temperature. We can experience all four seasons in one day. Before my administrative leave, I made mental memos that the detective's notes did not mention any cameras or recordings. What happened to them? The more I think about it, the more I realize I don't recall the exact details of Angel's magical evening with Mr. Maleeky Magic Dick. Knowing if there is video footage would give me more to work with. I am sure his cell phone was around. They could ping his phone or subpoena the provider to get more information. Not that I would want that. If that ping my phone, it will be easy to explain away my purpose in being there. Really simple. I was there because we are in a relationship of some sort. He tends to relate to other people, but yeah, we are in a relationship. Now if the cameras inside the house were rolling and someone has it in their possession, that will require a lot more thought and effort.

Being off from work, all I had was time; time to reflect on my life, my time with Bone, my time with Celeste and Wen. *Shit, shit, shit!* I had to keep my focus on Magic for now. I am still reluctant to contact an attorney or family until I can reconstruct precise details of that night. Maybe not too precise. That would send up a flag. A chilled glass of wine will do me fine right now.

White Zinfandel was the only thing in the wine cooler. I did not bother reaching for a clean glass. I grabbed the one that was in the sink yesterday. It was a glass Magic had given me. We celebrated one of his opportunities to take his business to the next level. He was the lowest responsible bidder for the City of Detroit Housing contract. He would be responsible for the demolition and restoration of condemned and abandoned homes. He loved to create memories. We created so many memories in a short period. We dined out mostly on weekdays, and one day, it was his treat. The next day, it was mine. We took short vacations to different Islands. We made love every day we were together. We made a baby! Now that's a night I remember all the details.

Magic was older, but he performed in the bedroom like a twenty-year-old man. His magic stick was in premier condition. His mouth was a masterpiece sent from the heavens. Every time we kissed, sparks left his tongue and ignited the flames of ecstasy. Our bodies moved in harmony to any song playing on Bluetooth. It was as if we were meant for each other. His smooth, freckled, fair skin glided all over my body. The magic potion of love and passion ran down my thighs. The sounds we made were like music to my ears. With each stroke, I whispered in his ear, which rested ever so gently against my lips, "You are my King…" When I whispered those words, his thrust got deeper and deeper. I ran my fingernails down his spine. Before he could climax, I finessed my way on top of his magic stick. He could feel my muscles grip his shaft. Magic matched my energy. With each contraction, his wand contracted back. It was as if our bodies were speaking to each other. He caressed my breasts while my body softly butterflied on top of his. Mounted on top of him, Magic's gentle hands grabbed mine and we intensely looked into each other's eyes. I wanted to say what my heart and body were feeling, but the power of our explosion hushed me. Pulling me closer, he said it! Maleeky Mr. Magic Richard said, "I love you, Nikki." It was at that moment our no-title relationship would go to a heightened level.

Interjecting my sarcasm and humor, "Tell me you love me when your sac is full." He understood what I meant but disregarded my comment. "I'll tell you when you deliver our baby." Joyfully, "Baby, what baby." Somehow, he knew he had planted a seed… the seed that neither of us would ever get a chance to see.

16

DISAPPEARING ACT

Zinfandel, Xanax, anything would be good right now to help take the edge off. The more I thought about Magic, the more I wished I had pulled myself away from the self-serving ungrateful son of a bitch. I am trying to convince myself that I have no emotions or attachment to a man who pretended to love me. The man who betrayed me. Even if that is his body somewhere in the fields of Macomb County, I wanted to feel like I did not care, but I could not. The range of emotions I feel is overwhelming. Drifting in a sea of emotions and thoughts, Sheila kept coming to mind.

Sheila disappeared for a while. There was no mention of her. There were signs of her. My recurrent stay at Magic's home compelled me to do more cleaning. He did not keep the inside as immaculate as the outside. Though it was comfortable. Ready to kick back and relax, I washed the clothes that I had on the night before and noticed his and her monogrammed bath towels. This was odd, considering Magic said no one lived with him. Trying not to lose my cool, I took into consideration that they were alleged business partners. Sheila's personal items inside his home were not suspect, but… My curiosity got the best of me. I picked up the phone to ask Jamison a couple of questions about Sheila.

"Hello, Jay." Jamison was a chill person, "What's up, Nik?" I started right in on the nature of my call. "Do you know if Sheila was ever a resident at Magic Island? I see monogrammed towels and other personal stuff. I have a sneaky suspicion; she is a frequent flyer. You know more than he let on." Jamison could not wait to tell me she knew of Sheila. Sheila graduated from Chadsey High School in Southwest Detroit with at least three of Jamison's closest friends, and Sheila was always talking about how much she does for Magic and that Magic Island was her property; he was there on borrowed time. Jamison recalled someone mentioning they planned to get married. Jamison let it be known that she sees Sheila often during holiday seasons. Sheila does a drive-by or two in the summer. "Nik, I did not tell you this stuff because I saw you falling hard for the guy. I figured you would find out soon enough and take flight." My jaw hit the floor. I am pregnant with a child and finding out Maleeky was a liar. If Sheila and Magic were still seeing each other, why was he pursuing me so hard? Why all the calls, the text, the lovemaking? What was his game plan? Whatever it was, an abortion was not an option for me. Guess I will be Sheila's wife-in-law. Magic was on his way back into the house, I hurriedly ended my conversation with Jamison, "Thanks, Jay, I'll talk to you soon."

And the Best Actor Award goes to (*drum roll*) … "Nikki featuring Mr. Magic." My line of work was stressful enough. I had to think about being a new mother. If there was more to it, Sheila would show her face again.

My reflections on the time spent with Maleeky at Magic Island kept me fixated on my encounters with Sheila. In Magic's version of Three Card Molly, Sheila is my number one pick as a suspect in his vanishing act.

17

CLOSE-UP

By this time, there were enough flags on Magic he could represent the United Nations. I held on. I wanted my child to have their father, their biological father, in their life. My own mother robbed me of the opportunity as a child. I was willing to accept Magic's stuff for that reason only. My position was knee-deep. Days went on, and I refrained from telling Magic I knew more than he thought. I kept the peace for the sake of our baby girl. We discussed names. I thought about naming her after me…Nikki. We agreed on another name…Star. Star was our baby girl's name. She would grow up and shine so brightly. She would reach for the stars. Star was going to make her parents proud. Having Star gave Magic and me a chance to be parents. We thought it was a blessing for both of us. I chose to stay positive and keep loving Magic. I supported his endeavors, but not his bullshit.

A passionate night of lovemaking and laughter turned into one of the scariest moments of my life. It was a blizzard outside. I called off work and decided to sleep in. Morning sickness was kicking in. Everything I tried to eat, Star rejected. Star was not fond of hot chocolate or waffles. I showered and went home to get in my bed. I was not feeling well. It did not seem like it was from morning sickness. It was an intuitive feeling telling me to get up and leave. I listened to my intuition.

The next morning, I called Magic and did not get an answer. That was not unusual, though. He must have forgotten I had my very first prenatal appointment scheduled. Magic was on board to go with me. Guessing he forgot the appointment was scheduled, so I showed up at his house. Surprise, Surprise! After making entry into the house, Sheila was on her knees pleasuring, Maleeky's dick. I was kind of impressed with her technique. If I had watched long enough, I would have learned something. She was given an A ++, based on the way only the whites of his eyes were visible. His pupils were somewhere in the back of his head. They were so into the moment neither one noticed my presence. When I turned to leave, Sheila pulled Magic's wand from her mouth so hard I could hear the gulping sound. The sounds of Magic's feet stomping on the floor were an indication he was furious. He was also conflicted. "NIKKI, WAIT!" Facing both with a grimacing expression, "Wait for Sheila to swallow your potion, or wait for you to get dressed so we can go to the doctor's office?" Sheila was stunned by the mention of the doctor's appointment, "Maleeky, what doctor's appointment? Are you sick? Do you got something?" Before Magic could respond, I told her, "No, Sheila, I'm pregnant with his baby. He got a baby in me." I could see the blood leave his magic wand. His penis shriveled like he just got out of a cold pool. "No worries, you two carry on." Sheila was in a fit of rage, "Magic, I thought you were going to get rid of her." Trying to subdue *Angel,* "Sheila, I'm going through that door, and Magic, you will never see me or Star again." Those words must have infuriated Magic because he turned his hostility towards Sheila. "Sheila, shut the fuck up before I kill you." That was a shocking comment, even for Magic. This whole scenario was not worth anyone getting hurt. Sheila blurted out, "Oh, you going to kill me too!" She carried on about how much she loved him and did not want to play second fiddle to some young bitch who did not understand their history together.

Kill me too… Who did he kill? What did Sheila know? Swarming with anxiety and exasperation, "Nobody is going to kill anyone. Sheila, Magic loves you. I will leave so you two can hash it out." Sheila insisted she had seen me there all summer long. I was there all summer long. But I was not going to tell the old bitty that. My goal was to exit through the door and not look back. Magic insisted that I was staying and not going anywhere. Too tired to fuss and think about Star, I went to the bathroom. Splashing cold water on my face, trying to ignore what I had just seen, I needed to get ready for my appointment. Looking in the mirror, I was promising myself I would swear off

Magic. This could not be my life right now. Here I am in the middle of a love tryst with Maleeky, Mr. Magic Dick! Listening from the bathroom, the two of them continued to squabble, barking back and forth with each other, and Sheila disappeared. I hoped it was for good this time.

18

FLOATING

Magic Island turned into Desert City. My mood was dry. The sounds of Sheila's cries replayed through my head. I was weak for Magic, and she was too. I tried to find humor in Sheila, taking a big gulp of Magic. There was none. I told Jamison I thought Sheila should have bent his wand backward. Because if it were *Angel*, she would tear the club up. The curtains would have died that night. Bone can attest to that. Betrayal is an unnecessary act. A simple conversation to let a person know you are moving on changes the dynamics. I felt betrayed by Magic as well. Positively, Sheila felt the same thing, if not worse. It was my understanding through Jamison they were college sweethearts. How sweet.

Maleeky's mess had him fired up. I was weary with frustrations. This was not going in a good direction. Celeste and Wendy would be disappointed if I told them. I wanted to tell them. They were unaware of my pregnancy status. I wanted to surprise them with a surprise invitation to a baby shower. I hopped in the shower, trying to relax, but I began to cramp. I ran the washcloth between my legs and noticed blood. I dropped the cloth and used my hand to swipe between my legs. There was more blood. Magic was cooking, singing, and dancing. I called out to him. He could not hear me. My voice fainted from shock. This could not be happening. I stepped out of the shower and wiped again. Only this time, there were clots. A clot was in the toilet. I sat there and cried. Sliding down the toilet, I balled up in a fetal position. Weeping and wailing. My Star, my baby, was in the toilet.

Magic heard my cries and entered the bathroom, "Nikki, get up. What's wrong?" I pointed to the toilet. He barely looked. He walked back into the kitchen. I cleaned up, and we sat in silence. Magic kissed my forehead, "Baby, we will try again and again." I regrouped so Magic could take me to the hospital. I blew a kiss to Star before flushing the toilet. That was the last of my baby. I cried like one, too.

19

ATTRACTION

Magic gravitated to women and money. Specifically, women with money. He was a hermit on the surface. Contrary to appearances, he enjoyed the spotlight. He enjoyed entertaining large crowds. Entertainment was the attraction for Magic. The world was his stage. Everyone around him was an actor in his production. My friends thought Magic had a creep factor about him. Contrary to their opinions, the more I discovered about him, the more attracted I was to his illusive eeriness.

Jamison called me from the parking lot of the grocery store in Lincoln Park. Magic was flirting with a lady inside. At first, Magic rubbed the lady the wrong way, and then, somehow, the script flipped. I was imagining how the scene was playing out. Her initial impression of him was annoyed by his persistent persuasions. Then he said something to make her panties drop. He flashed a smile, then poof…Magic!

Jamison was familiar with the lady. She did not live in the area but frequented the area. She sang in jazz clubs and performed side gigs for various artists. Her name was Leidy. Jamison gave me a description of "Leidy Sings the Blues" and the type of car she drives. Leidy drove a gold Audi. She wore an Afghan and brown shoes. An Afro-centric vibe. Jamison thought her style had a voodoo vibe. I let out a snicker and visualized the description Jamison gave me, "But of course." Jamison was always signifying someone was into voodoo, based on their appearance. She called some of our fellow officers Voodoo King and Queen.

Weeks after the notification from Jamison, I noticed Magic was staying out all night. He lied about his whereabouts. He did not owe me an explanation, but he offered up lies. Lies that fell on deaf ears. I started to feel the pullback. Magic and Leidy were doing things that hinted that their canoodling was not an ordinary rendezvous. This was love between the two of them. I may have had him physically, but she had his heart and beyond.

I wanted to see her. I could feel her energy all over him. Magic's vernacular started to change. He started using the greeting Namaste; I bow to the God/King or Queen in you. He cleaned the house more. He even wanted to give up his pipe. I applauded her infectious influence on Magic. He was not this enthusiastic about getting Star's nursery together. Any project he started he left half done. He always complained that it was a lack of money to finish the job. I would give him money. Magic misappropriated the money I gave him. My savings dwindled, trying to help him through a rough patch. Meanwhile, I stayed at my place crying the blues.

Leidy had a sex appeal that drew Magic in. His attitude towards me became cold. Downright mean. I went from being his Buttercup to his Bitch. My presence irritated him. Magic got rid of any physical signs of me being in his house. The first thing I noticed; he removed my painting from the wall. Magic changed his look. He was becoming more interested in his style of dress. He was buying more suits.

#2

CABARET

I was no longer going to be the magician's assistant. The gig was over. It was time for a night out with the ladies. Out of all the places to choose from, my friends chose to hang out at a free jazz concert off the water. I did not want to hear any jazz. I forced myself to go out. Hangtown was near the Downriver area, so we made our way to the jazz concert on the river. Lo and behold, I spotted Magic and Leidy. She was preparing to perform. How wonderful! Magic never saw me with my friends. When Leidy stepped away to perform, Magic started dialing my phone. Quickly, I turned it down so he could not hear his special ringtone.

Stepping further away into another area of the park, I watched him watch her perform and look over his shoulder. Magic was unfamiliar with my inner circle. He thought he had secrets. My circle was kept under wrap due to the nature of my line of work. As an officer and investigator living in the jurisdiction in which I worked, I could not risk my world being identified. I was especially cautious about introducing anyone who worked in a special task force or plainclothes officers. You never know if you will have a drink with someone one day and arrest them the next.

#3

SPECTATOR FAILURE

Days, weeks, and hours went by. I was still off work, and the local news had not released any updates on Magic's case. The County Coroner had a backlog of bodies, but geesh. I was becoming desperate. The torment gave me insomnia. I still refuse to talk to anyone. Not even Celeste and Wendy. I need more intel before making a statement. I mean, come on, I know they do not think I would rat myself out. I am not ratting *Angel* out, either. Magic is high profile. He should have moved to the top of the list of things for the Medical Examiner to do. The longer it takes, the more time I have… to piece over all the details.

I am sticking to my list of suspects. Sheila, Leidy, or *Angel*. All three have motives. People rarely commit random acts of crime. Usually, it is money, power, and respect. You can throw love in there somewhere. A person's love for money- greed, love for power- control, or love of respect- appreciation. See, Sheila was a money motive, Leidy wanted control over Magic and the Island, then Angel wanted respect. Sometimes, all of the above are motivations. Magic's charm would be his downfall.

For every lie he sold me, I pretended to buy it. He thought I was greener than the artificial lawn in his yard. I warned Magic to stop sending me pictures of his concubine. I was not impressed by his collection of women. I also warned him to stop trying to do the bait and switch. That old-school nonsense was hilarious to me. It is when a guy will call you and give you another woman's name and harp on

63

that particular woman, making it seem as though he is interested in said woman; all the while, he is hooking up with someone else. That was a major flag, and I was throwing flags on his play.

20

INVULNERABILITY

Refusing to be vulnerable to Magic, I began to curtail my feelings for him. His arrogance and subliminal remarks about all his female friends carrying guns or his work for mobsters were ridiculously insane to me. Did he think that would keep Angel or Nikki away? Laughable. Not that I'm invincible, but the ladies I saw hanging around Magic Island did not seem like a suitable challenge for me or Angel, for that matter. I was confused by the sudden change in his loveable nature. He was turning grim.

I was too outdone when I realized their connection was spiritual. They had kindred spirits. I naturally touched his heart and soul with a supernatural power called love. Leidy forced a connection through gimmicky persuasion and ceremonial traditions. I could not knock her for it. It was working. He drank the potion and soon forgot about me. Magic was not himself. Maleeky, Mr. Magic Richard, was disappearing right before my very eyes.

Maleeky thought I was spying on him. I never had to. My vibration was high, and he was seen in various places by people I know. I did not want them to tell me, yet they did. Besides, his guilty conscience told on himself. Either that, or he was trying to tell me in so many ways that I was no longer the object of his affection. The absence of direct communication is highly undesirable. Avoidance is a major disturbance for me. Face your truth no matter what the consequences are!

I discerned they were performing a cord-cutting ritual with candles I bought for Magic and me to have a candlelight dinner. My wick was lit! A cord-cutting ritual characteristically severs the energetic ties you share with another. It is symbolic of cutting ties with people, places, or anything you no longer desire or have an interest in. I could not believe my eyes! Then again, yes, I could. Parts of me knew Magic did not have my best interest. Angel, on the other hand, was livid and ready to wrap that cord around their necks!

Smoke was steaming off the top of my skull! Magic and *Leidy Singing the Blues* would feel the wrath of *Angel*. Leidy involved herself where she did not belong. Angel did not want to give Leidy the blues, but trying to convince Magic that Nikki had negative energy was absurd. Magic is the one who built up the façade that we were going to do life together. After losing Star we continued to try for another baby. Marriage was not on the table for either of us. Neither of us gave marriage consideration. Magic had never been married, but knowing marriage was a piece of paper that binds couples financially did not impress me. I found it impressive to watch Magic turn his magic performance into a circus show, juggling three women at a time. I forewarned Magic there were parts to me he never wanted to see. My sixth sense was one thing, but *Angel* is an expert at her craft.

21

EXTRASENSORY PERCEPTION (ESP)

A true magician never reveals their tricks. Keep your audience guessing. One thing that I did not share with anyone was I was born with a veil over my face. Biologically, that meant the film from the amniotic sac covered my face. According to my mother, spiritually, it means the Great I AM is protecting me from any hurt, harm, or foul. A shield from the unknown. No weapon formed will prosper and the offender would experience supernatural karma right before my very eyes. Simply put, I am human, but there is a spirit in me that lives in me that takes care of me. My gift of discernment and intuition heads danger off before it manifests.

My intuition guided me. Angel protected me. Angel is carnal. Angel is an extension of Nikki. Angel is not an imaginary friend or a separate identity of Nikki. Although I felt like she was a special friend that no one wanted to meet. Angel is Nikki's defender. Angel filled the void that I missed growing up without my father. When I said I knew there was a difference in me, that difference was my ability to look deeper into myself to protect me from the things my mother and stepfather could not protect me from. They could not protect me from me. They could not protect me from the damage that was established at birth. The Lies that replayed in my head were something I struggled with; literally every conversation Terry and I had, I dissected it, trying to figure out what was fact and what was a lie! I do not have blackouts or amnesia when Angel shows up. I am fully aware and cognizant of what Angel does. Nikki is *Angel. Angel* is Nikki. I am her.

How could I trust anyone if the one person I should be able to trust, my mother Terry, could look me in the eyes, the world for that matter, and tell me that the man she entrusted to play the role of a father was not my biological father? For crying aloud, she was married. My biological father was married to someone else. His wife did not know of my existence. The betrayal had deep layers of betrayal. Searching for that truth, searching for my identity, was something that a child should not have had to experience. Terry told me who my father was, but it was too late to develop any kind of friendship or parent/child relationship. A missed opportunity. Little inconspicuous details of my life were kept from me. God forbid I inherited a genetic disorder from my biological father. For all I know, Angel could be a symptom of dissociative identity disorder, and mental illness could be a paternal trait.

Imagine Star was born, and something was wrong with her; who would I go to for answers? My biological father is deceased. I will have to do an ancestry test to find my family. Would the family welcome me? Would they want to know me? For Pete's sake, whenever I start a family, they would only get to have a piece of me and not the whole extension of me. Unfair!

Terry delegated Benny Harris to fulfill the role, but he was a poor actor. I felt the divide between him and me. The Harris family was not warm and receiving of me either. The air was so thick when I went to Harris' family gatherings by the time I was ten years old, I could sense I was different. The constant reminders that my physical features were different from theirs, were impressed upon my brain. The awkwardness I felt when Benny showed up for my siblings, but not for me. I carried a name that did not rightfully belong to me. I wanted my true lineage. In the same way, slave masters gave their slaves names that did not belong to them, and this was the captivity of a lifelong lie. It was a perpetual sense of doom.

These were emotions and feelings I did not disclose to anyone. In the back of my mind, I knew Angel would comfort me. She would take care of me. I had to lean on Angel every time a person let me down. For me, it is not the act of betrayal that slices through the heart like a Samurai sword, but the lies told to cover the act. The mere fact that someone will cause another person to be hurt by covering their own dirt hurts worse than any truth revealed. The truth was not upsetting.

Whatever means a person subscribes to dealing with life, it's considered coping. Be it good or bad. Some turn to substance use, they go to therapy, they rely on religion, and that's life. We do not get to choose how someone reacts to our actions! *Angel* is reactionary.

I blasted the music from Stevie Wonder's album Hotter Than July. I hummed the lyrics to *Rocket Love*. My relationship with Magic was coming to a screeching halt, and the separation was a familiar space. First Sheila, now Leidy. Afraid to dare think there could be more.

Throwing up in my own mouth at the images in my cornea, Magic loved to perform oral and give deep-throat kisses. Yuck at the thought. He put that precious mouth on Leidy's lips between her hips and then kissed me. It was unimaginable. It did not make sense. A nightmare, a freaking nightmare! Here, I am on administrative leave, trying to sort through a mess. It would have been so much easier had I never involved myself with Maleeky.

At the end of the day, they are going to blame all of this on Nikki, not *Angel*, not anyone else, but me, Nikki! The harder I tried to escape my childhood trauma, the more I fell into the cycle of that trauma. Magic coddled me and took me under his wing. He held me tight at night and rubbed my back until I fell asleep. Now, just like that, instead

of communicating with me honestly…, ♫ *"You Took Me Riding…,"* continuing to sing the Stevie Wonder jam, I could relate to every word of this song. Tears streamed down my face. There was a downpour outside my window from the rain and inside my home from my tears.

Time was closing in. To soothe my conscience, I decided to call Celeste and Wendy first. Then I will call Bone, and next, I will call my attorney. Reconciling Magic Maleeky Dick is dead, and I very well may be responsible for his death. I was ready to make a statement and turn myself in. Though, I left him at Magic Island, there alive. I never experienced a blackout, but with *Angel* by my side, who knows what happened between the time I left and returned to check on him.

22

VANISH

The weather was chilly for early September in Michigan. It was sixty-five degrees. My heart was racing from all the tricks Magic played on me. He created the illusion that we were going to have a blissful life together. How could I fall for the charade? Revenge was not what I was after. I wanted Magic to look me in the eye and tell me that he wanted to cut the cord, and it was not Leidy wanting him to cut the cord. Magic needed to be responsible and tell me that everything he said to me inside the bedroom and out was not a lie. He owed me that much.

Unbeknownst to Magic, I had a silent investor on deck ready to front me $2 million dollars. That was less than what I needed to launch my new business. It was enough to loan Magic for his upgrades for Mr. Magic's Restoration. He needed employees to assist him with some upcoming contracts. I already accepted the money and relied on us working together as a team. After seeing Leidy was a frequent flyer and not going anywhere, I wanted to know if we were in this thing together or not. I could easily return any unused portion of the money and go on with my life. The only problem was the silent investor was looking for a 9.9 % return on investment. He was confident I would seal a deal with Magic and make good on the return on investment. He thought we could franchise Magic's handy services. Now, I had to rework my whole plan.

I grabbed the keys off the counter and headed to the garage. I had said it many times before, but I was through with Magic, and obviously, he was through with me. My heart was palpitating. I wanted to stay calm. I wanted this to be a closure conversation. I wanted to understand what was happening between us.

When I parted from my ex-husband, he understood without having to guess why I was moving on. I closed the door and did not look back. That is what mature, rational adults do, right? They close and lock the freaking door! Anxiety was kicking in. I had forgotten to take my Xanax.

We live a short distance away from each other. A ten-minute drive felt like half an hour. Atlantic Star's classic played in the background on the radio a hundred times *If Your Heart Isn't In It.* Why was Maleeky making this complicated? Scantily dressed in a three-quarter length black raincoat, with a purple lace teddy underneath and high-heeled shoes, I parked my 1969 purple Mustang into his driveway. I brought the Mustang out of storage for special occasions. This was one of them.

Magic was on the telephone. I could hear him through the door. I waited outside for his call to end. I could hear the smile in his voice. Waiting a few more minutes, pulling out the burner phone from my raincoat, I dialed Magic's phone to see if he would answer. He told the person, "Hang on a minute, it is Nikki calling me. Do not worry. I will get rid of her." Was he serious? Magic was clicking on the other line to answer my call, and I was standing right behind him. Startled, "NIKKI WHAT THE FUCK ARE YOU DOING HERE. WHY DIDN'T YOU CALL FIRST." Ignoring his aggression, I walked past him and went straight to his bedroom. The smell of cheap perfume was lingering in the room. Guessing Leidy just left, and he was talking to her on her drive home. "Calm down, Magic, and let Nikki put these magic hands on you and massage your shoulders." I wiggled my fingers in the air, suggesting my hands were about to do magic. Magic gave me a once over, and his eyes lit up. Magic wrapped his arms around my waist and gave me a peck on the lips. Sliding off the raincoat and lingerie but leaving on the heels, I teased him with a dance and pushed him onto the bed. My body moved in unison to the soft music Magic was playing. My index finger touched his nose and slid down to his lips. He gently bit my finger. His soft hands rubbed me all over. Reaching in between his thighs to feel his magic wand and…

POOF NOTHING! No erection. That was not like Magic. He was able to cum and have an erection seconds later. Now, I was certain Leidy was there prior to me. She must have zapped all his juices. Trying to ignore that his body was not responding to mine, I gave him a bonus. Reaching in my trick bag for the whipped cream, squirting a couple of drops in my mouth, Magic got the royal edition of oral. My tongue flickered across the head of his penis, and moving my tongue as if I had a mouth full of marbles, I took the whole thing down my throat, slowly sliding it out and licking my lips. I told him how good he tasted. Wiping the cream from the corners of my mouth, I massaged his thighs with my lips and gently blew on his sac. I could feel the blood rushing to his wand, and I was blowing his mind, "Nikki, what are you doing to me?" With a soft reply, "Turn on your stomach, Maleeky."

Magic never caught on to me calling him by his government name when I was serious with him. No games, no jokes. It was business in the bedroom tonight. Nikki had a trick to perform. Magic did not know there was a razor between my teeth and tongue. I nicked his magic wand, nothing deep, superficial tiny cuts. The blood rituals between him and Leidy kept him from having a sensational effect. Removing the razor from my mouth, I placed it in the bun of my braids. I sat my wet pussy on his tailbone and leaned forward to kiss the back of his neck and shoulders. Magic started to feel the warmth rushing from the cuts. The blood was seeping out from his penis. It probably felt like paper cuts. That's exactly what I intended. He tried to flip over, but my weight kept him pressed to the bed. Pulling his silky ponytail, I yanked his head towards me. He was facing the mirrored headboard. I wanted him to look in the mirror and see me sitting on his back, reaching for the razor in my bun. His body twisted and turned, attempting to buck me off his back. With tears falling, "Relax, Magic, the more you fight, the worse it gets." I did not want to kill him, but *Angel* swelled up inside, and for the first time, I heard *Angel's* voice, *"Do it, Nikki, or he will kill you."* Suppressing Angel's command. My eyes were still piercing at Magic, watching me through the mirror. Teasing and taunting him, "I thought you liked it bloody." With the grace of a ballet dancer, I pressed my knee into his back and stretched the other leg behind me. With one hand gripping his hair, I grabbed the razor from my bun and began to…hear my phone ring.

My burner phone rang. Only one person had the number. Not answering because I was in the middle of showtime with Magic, but it rang again. If Bone called back-to-back, it meant there was something important going on. Raising off Magic and against my better judgment, I answered, "Bone, what's up?" Bone was talking, and I was keeping my eye on Magic. "Nikki, I need you to pick me up from the airport." Why was he at the airport in the first place? He was already here in Hangtown, bringing me the news of the streets talking. Now he is at the airport. Trying not to give him details, "Bone, I am busy. I told you I am in the middle of showtime with Magic." Bone was not stupid. If he has any kind of recollection, then he should remember showtime is when Angel is at her peak performance. Disregarding my anxiousness, Bone uncompromisingly, "Nikki be at the airport in twenty minutes!" Gazing over at Maleeky, I lit his pipe and blew the smoke in his face. My whole act was to show him if he wanted to play tricks with my mind, Angel would dispel the trickery.

Astonishingly, that was the first time I saw him speechless. "Hmmmm, nothing to say, Mr. Magic?" Quiet as a church mouse. With teardrops gushing down his face, Magic shook his head in disbelief. In the same way, I shook my head in disbelief at his juvenile antics. The guy was in his fifties, still playing games and misleading women. Walking away was too easy. Maleeky Dick has gotten away with this one too many times. He attempted to bite me when I tied the scarf around his mouth. "Now, now, you need to behave like a good boy. This will not be long; I am going to pick up a friend. Do not fret if anyone calls. I will have your cell with me." With no time to waste. Dragging him to his panic room and placing his cell phone in my pocket simultaneously, "If your Leidy calls, I will let her leave you a voicemail. You can call her back in the morning." I left Maleeky there. After I pick up Bone, I will return to finish the job. I was not through with Magic.

Picking Bone up from the airport is biting off more than I could chew. Taking the freeway to the Metro Airport from Hangtown was going to be at least half an hour. That's too much time to leave Magic in the house unattended. He may escape or, even worse, bleed out. Whew, *breathe, Nikki, breathe.* I had to tell myself to breathe. I was no longer in Angel mode. Good Lord, what have I done? Too late to think about that. I needed to think of what I was going to do to recover. I'm at the point of no return. I mean, even if he is alive when I get back, Magic would never let that shit go. He is not Bone. Like Angel said, he would kill me. I am going to have to tell Bone that my performance on the Island was a flop.

I did not like holding it over Bone's head, but after that gun, he put to my head, he was indebted to me for life. I will always call in favors. Thank goodness I had extra clothes at Magic's house. The temperature started to drop. I could hear Bone asking why I was stepping out with nothing but lingerie on. I got closer to the airport and started checking Magic's cell. I wanted to make sure he did not get any important texts or calls that needed an immediate response. I already did my homework. Leidy had a gig later that night, and Sheila was on a family vacation. Besides, Leidy had just left Magic Island before her gig. Hopefully, she did not forget anything or expect Magic to show up. I pulled into the domestic pick-up lane and saw Bone standing there with a motorcycle jacket and flicking a Newport cigarette. When did he start smoking? His nerves must be shot. Bone was not a drinker or smoker. He hated it. I believe it was due to his parents being substance abuse users. That was one of the only conscientious choices he made.

Before I could completely stop, Bone snatched the passenger side door of my Mustang open. Now he knew I was going to raise holy hell about that, "Fool, what's wrong with you snatching on my door? I just got that paint job, and you interrupting some very important stuff!" With an attitude, "I know Nikki, I know, just take me to the Motel off Northline Rd. in Southgate. I gotta lay low for a minute." He could hear the irk in my jerk, switching to fifth gear, "First of all, what do you mean you know? Secondly, lay low for what?" Bone was sitting there non-responsive. Not dead, but he was not talking. Doing at least 75 mph all the way there, we got there in less than fifteen minutes.

Again, before stopping, he flung the door open. Bone was on one, and so was I. I needed to get back to my concert at Magic Island.

#4

Contemplating what I was going to do with Magic, I opted to take my car home and ride my bicycle back to his place. I could call Bone to help with cleaning up after he gets done with whatever he was working with. The temperature in his house was freezing cold, but it was slightly chilly outside, but not cold enough for the inside to feel like an icebox. Taking baby steps to the panic room, I noticed the panic door was wide open. Before I looked inside the panic room, I thought it was best to start peddling back towards the exit door. Magic was probably hiding somewhere in the house, waiting to pick me off with his AR-15. I grabbed my .40 caliber from my holster and used the Alexa to turn the lights on throughout the house. The house was spic and span, and I wasn't there to clean it. Looking at the camera app, there was nothing but a black screen. Yelling out for Magic to come on out, I surrender, "Magic… come out, come out wherever you are." We were now in a game of hide and seek. Checking the closets and walking into the living room, checking behind the sofa, I checked the guest room bathrooms and then went to the panic room, Magic was gone! Not a word! Not a sound. No Magic! The inside was spotless, and Magic's dog Teddy was gone too!

Angel was stepping in for Nikki, "Come out, mother fucker! It's showtime!" Still, nothing! Should I leave or stay? Wait for Magic to return. No way, I was getting the hell out of there and calling Bone.

23

SYMPATHETIC REACTION

My legs were tired from cycling back to my house. I was pumping the bike so hard and fast that you would have thought I was a professional cyclist. I made it to my house, practically falling out on the lawn. The bike was coming inside with me. Everyone and their mother had a ring doorbell camera, so breaking the bike down was a lot easier than trying to get rid of my Mustang. I removed my all-black tracksuit and shoes. Those were going in the trash. I could not call off work. That was too obvious. I was there and now he's not. I tortured him. Now he's gone. His phone had not rung either. If Leidy came back to rescue him, I'm in deep shit. They certainly would report everything to Internal Affairs. Staring at the wall, my burner rang. Good, it was Bone. I was going to tell him we must meet up and talk. "Hey Bone, you..." Trying to finish my sentence when he interrupted me, "Nikki, what are you doing? Celeste and Wendy keep calling me. You need to call them. They said your work and personal lines are going straight to voicemail." Damn, what could they want? I thought they were working with extra sensory perception (ESP). Wen and Celeste were highly intuitive, too. Their guts must have told them I was up to something. "Okay, Bone, I will call."

This time, I called Wendy first. I could explain things better to Wen without all the melodrama that Celeste would bring. They were on speed dial. "What's up, Wendy?" There was a long silence. Dang, did she hear about Magic already? Was the po-po's coming for me? All kinds of things traveled through my brain in between our silence, "Wen, what is it?" Not that I care now, "Wen, sis, what's wrong?" Wendy's voice crackled, "It's momma, Terry..." Lord, "What did she do now?" "Nikki, momma is dead, she's dead, Nikki, Terry is gone.

My momma is gone." Listening to Wen cry, my jaw hit the floor before my body dropped. I almost passed out. "What! What happened!" My eyes would not let me cry. My heart seemingly stopped. This was horrible news, but also a good reason for me to call off tomorrow. Now I had to deal with this and Magic's vanishing act. "Does Celeste know?" "Yes, Nikki, she knows we both were trying to call you. When we could not get a hold of you, we had Rod reach out to Bone." Stunned, dazed, downright mummified, this was hell to tell the captain." Literally. "Okay, Wen, let me call my Lieu and let him know I will be taking some p.t.o. time, are you and Celeste flying in as soon as possible?" "Of course, Nikki, I mean damn…you live right in the state with her, and the neighbors had to call us to tell us she had a massive heart attack, so yes, Nikki, we will be flying in and handling the arrangements." "Bye, Wendy." Wendy was talking to me like I did not have my reasons for not talking to Terry. Me not talking to her did not mean I wanted anything to happen to her. She was my mother, too. There was nothing she could have said that would make me feel like denying me a right to know and having a relationship with my biological father was in my best interest.

#2

I called Lieutenant Chap on his work cell. His shift was over, "Lieu, this is Detective Harris." Grumpy Lieutenant Chap, "I know who you are. I am looking at the caller ID" "Lieu, my mother passed away, and I would like to use five days of bereavement for time off, sir." With compassion in his otherwise facetious manner, "Nik, I am deeply sorry to hear this. Take as much time as you need. I will let the police union and chaplain know. Take care of yourself, Detective Harris." Lieu's show of sympathy means a lot to me right now. If a hard nose like Lieu's can offer me compassion in my time of need, why was it so hard for me to forgive Terry?

Bone got the word on Terry through the grapevine, better known as Celeste and Wendy. The day was filled with calls of care and concern. I was in a fake it til' I made it mode. Here, I am preparing to bury my mother. The woman who birthed me, yet I did not speak to her for years. Selfishly, I never asked the questions of how I, Nikki, the love child came to be. I was too wrapped up in my own clouded mind to entertain the idea that something drove her through the door into the arms of another man. None of that matters now. Terry, my dear mother…

Figuratively, Magic's blood was on my hands. But in the words of Detective Hollis, *suck it up, Buttercup.*" Wendy and Celeste were on their way through the door. They took the first thing smoking from Texas and Florida to get to Michigan. Keith was going to do the eulogy. Rod was already here in Michigan, taking care of business.

I was excited to see my niece and nephews. "Come here, KKK. When they are all together, I would call them that. Their first initials are "K"- Keith Jr. Kyle and my niece Kam'ron. Happy to see their Aunt Nikki, they ran to me and embraced me with the warmest hugs. I held Kam'ron so tight. Tears streaming down my eyes. I wanted to be a mother and seeing her made me think of what my twinkling little Star would be like. If only Magic could have seen the twinkle in my eyes for him, we would have been a great family. Tickling KKK, we giggled and smiled. My smile was masking all the pain I felt inside. The fear of what's to come.

#3

BROKEN WAND

Three days later, we had Terry's funeral. The church was filled with officers, neighborhood friends, Bone, Rod's and Keith's extended family. The whole gambit was there. Benny Harris, my stepfather, was there in a show of support for his daughters. Standing over the casket, so many memories reran. I watched the slide show that played on the projector above my mother's casket. This was it. The end of Terry and me. My mother and I had not talked in over five years, and right then and there, I wanted to talk. I wanted to tell her I forgave her. My emotions were overwhelming me. What better time than now to let her know I forgive her? This was a harsh reality for me. A bitter pill to swallow. The fact that I was here on this earth would not change. The circumstances would not change. The only thing that could have changed was how I responded to the news. This was true for the other situations in my life as well.

The time was now for me to accept *Angel* would no longer be my protector. I wasn't a little girl anymore. *Angel* was causing more harm than good. She lashed out. She was not a voice of reason or forgiveness. Sweeping things under the rug was not forgiving. Acknowledging my hurt and finding a positive way to deal with it would be the change I needed. I discussed extensively the issue of individuals not being held accountable for their actions. I never discussed being accountable for the reaction. Angel was the reactionary side of me. I would have to acknowledge my reaction to being hurt did not warrant some of the things Angel did. Though it gave momentary satisfaction, usually someone was going to be hurt. They would hurt worse than the pain I originally felt. *Angel* was not healthy for Nikki. *Angel* was not helping me cope but a justification to show the world how angry I was. *Angel* was fierce. I was weary with grief. Grieving the loss of my unborn child, grieving the loss of my mother, grieving the loss of Magic, grieving my impending separation from Angel. For me to not become all the things I despised about Terry, I was going to have to release my grief and take culpability for the torture and possibly death of Magic.

Deep into my epiphany, there was a tap on my shoulder. It was Sgt. Smitty. He grabbed my hand and escorted me outside the church. With a disturbed look on my face, "What is it, Smitty? I'm having a moment with Terry, in case you had not noticed." "Nikki, a female by the name of Leidy DeJournette, walked into the station and reported, a Maleeky Richard missing."

Where's Xanax when you need it? The service could not finish soon enough. Leidy reporting him missing is insane. Why did Magic's family not report him missing? I couldn't bail at my mother's funeral. However, I wanted to. Celeste and Wendy kept turning their heads to see what was happening. I still have not told them about the Magic Island ordeal and do not plan on it… just yet. When the service is over, they will have to stay in a hotel or take their things to my mother's house. She lived in Southwest Detroit. Not too far from Hangtown.

That would give them a chance to start going through her things. There was too much for me to manage. Having kids over and folks drinking, going down memory lane about all the stuff Terry used to say and do…I could not handle that. Not after knowing Magic was officially reported missing.

24

PHYSICAL ANOMALY

It's been almost a whole month of being on administrative leave. Days turned into weeks. My body was going through changes. Nothing I ate agreed with me. Xanax was no longer helping me sleep. Processing the events of Magic and the death of my mother was an anomaly. My eyes were seeing things, my ears were hearing things, but my core was going through the motions. I struggled to do everything, including brushing my teeth.

God was speaking directly to me in this moment. I did not have to open a bible. I clearly heard: *For we wrestle not against flesh and blood, but against principalities, against power, against the rulers of the darkness of this world, against spiritual wickedness in high places.*

Wrestling with my hurt and unforgiveness brought more wrath to me than anyone else. The way I chose to cope emphatically hurt others made me feel *Angel* was justified in her revenge on others. My intentions were to never hurt anyone, the same could be said for Terry. The same for Magic, Bone, me and my ex-husband. I did not need *Angel* to avenge their sins or slights against me. I needed to release them and walk away. I needed to forgive them. I needed to forgive myself. It sounded cliché. It was the only way I could free my soul.

For every action, there is a reaction. That was Newton's Third Law of Motion. It was the law for my emotions, period. It was the law! When one object exerts force on another object, the second object exerts an equal and opposite force. It was something I lived by. It was karmic. The energy you put out is the energy you get in return. The rule of physics, the rule of law, would have to apply to me as well.

For every offense, there is a charge. There is a consequence. I am going to have to face those consequences. If it means turning myself in. It's what I must do. They can blame it on Nikki. Magic's family did not need to bear any suffering at the hands of me. We all have darkness that will come to light. How I shine my light is what matters. Who I shine my light on is what counts. I'm shining my light on me. I won't use *Angel* as my defense.

#2

LET THE SHOW BEGIN

I checked to make sure my bath water was not overflowing. I did not bother eating, but the feeling of starvation was killing me. I had to try to eat something. The orange on the table should suffice. I peeled the orange and headed to the tub. Eating that orange in a warm bath with Epsom salt was so relaxing. I felt better about the idea of turning in my badge and writing out my statement. My appointment with the defense attorney, Sidney Farrington, is at 10 am. I wish it were earlier, but Sid was known for not being a morning person. She could hear me best after 9 am.

I dried myself off with the Egyptian cotton towel. Ohhh, it felt so good. Sitting there naked, trying to figure out what I will slide on to wear to my appointment with Sid. I heard a car pull into my driveway. I did not bother to check the camera app on my phone. Whoever it is, either using the driveway to turn around or coming to tell me I'm officially a suspect. Getting up to stretch, I sighed with relief. My doorbell rang!

25

RESTORATION

My jeans and sweatshirt were lying on top of the hamper. I slid those on. Rushing to the door, but not in a rush to see who it was, I picked up the phone to call Sid. "Hello Sid, this is Nikki. You know the things we discussed earlier…" "Hey, Nikki…yes, we have a meeting at 9 am. You have your statement, and you are prepared to speak with the media, right?" There was a knock at the door, thinking this was my 'heads up' from Shagwell. Talking with Sid anxiously, "Someone is at the door. I want you to be on standby in case they are here to arrest me." Reminding me to calm down and relax, "Nikki, you know how this goes. At worse, you are a suspect. The body has not been confirmed yet. At least, not to my knowledge. You know I get all the tea from my sources. Chill out. Against my better judgment, you are the one who wants to come forth in a stroke of consciousness to implicate yourself; right now, you sound temporarily insane. See who's at the door, and don't make any confessions or answer any questions. The only statement you will make is to inform them you have retained an attorney. They can speak to me." Whoever was on my porch was pacing back and forth. I could see the shadow, and it was only one person, so that's a good sign. "Okay, Sid, talk to you soon."

#2

MAGIC TRICK REVEALED

Placing my hand on the doorknob and unlocking the bolt lock. The knob twisted, but not from my force; the person on the other side was turning the knob. My heart was racing, beating like a drum at an African Music Festival. Don't tell me this is Magic. Cracking the door to catch a glimpse…Stunned with disbelief. I felt faint and dizzy.

Dazed and indifferent, it must be bad news, "ELLIS!" It was my ex-husband, Ellis. Ellis is a Commander in the neighboring jurisdiction. I was more than shocked to see him. Scared almost. Ellis grabbed me tight, "Nikki, I apologize for not making it to Terry's funeral. You have my condolences." Still overwhelmed by his presence, "Thanks, Ellis. I was on my way out. I have something I need to take care of." "Nikki, sit down for a minute. I took care of things for you, darling."

What did he mean by that? Did someone see something? In a world of cameras and doorbell cameras, that could not be ruled out. Ellis went on to explain, "The night you were at Magic Island, I was there to do a side job for Rod. I had to call Bone because your cell was going to voicemail. Bone is your ace, and I know you answer the phone for him day or night. So, I called him to ask you to pick him up from the airport. When you left, I went in. I cleaned up the mess you made. Then, I took care of Magic and his dog. Nikki, the body they recovered in Clinton Township is not Magic's. They will never find Magic or his dog. I removed the cameras and dismantled the whole system; I had his phone wiped. I figured you would pick it up and take it with you. My resources at the cell company removed your calls and texts from the server, too. Whatever you do, Nikki, you were not there. I was not there. Don't worry about any neighbors. The scrambler adjusted date/time stamps on their cameras. As far as anyone knows, Magic vanished and is considered missing. That's all, nothing else. Behave yourself, Nikki and put this behind you. They need you on the force, darling."

My ears are on fire. My heart was sinking. Ellis took care of Magic for Rod? Relieved that Angel or I was not responsible for his death but confused as to why Ellis was taking on a job for Rod. "Ellis, why?" In the typical, the less is the best way, "Nikki, sometimes it's best not to ask questions. That has always been your problem. You dig for answers you don't want the answer to. Things are not going to change. You have been on a quest for the truth since Terry told you Benny was not your father. Every time you go searching, you get more than your little heart can handle, so let this be. I love you girl. Always have, always will."

SIMPLY MAGICAL

Throwing up all over the place. I had uneasiness in my stomach, so I asked Ellis to leave so I could clean myself up. I had to call Sid and let her know we would still meet at her office, but there was a change of plan. I was going to wait for the call from Internal Affairs, hopefully I will return to work soon.

It's been almost eight weeks, and I still did not have my period. Oh, snap, I need a pregnancy test. Grabbing my keys and rushing through the door, I went to the pharmacy and bought a pregnancy test. Hopefully, stress is making me late. I can't imagine what life will be like having Magic's baby and he is not here to see the baby. Sidney is going to get a hoot out of this! I'll take the test in her office. I recited a scripture to myself Terry frequently reminded me of, *"Let no one deceive himself. If anyone among you seems to be wise in this age, let him become a fool that he may become wise. For the wisdom of this world is foolishness with God. For it is written, "He catches the wise in their own craftiness."*

The radio was blasting, Rochelle Ferrell's-*I Forgive You*. I was about to uncomplicate my life and forgive myself. No more *Angel*.

AUDIENCE ENGAGEMENT

1. Sheila mentions, "Kill me too." Would you like to know who Magic killed?

2. Ellis is the ex-husband. Why do you think Nikki's brother-in-law, Rodd, reached out to him to "take care" of Magic?

3. Nikki talks about her ex briefly; do you think they ended on bad terms? Was he familiar with Angel?

4. Are Bone and Nikki trauma bonded or truly have a deep love for each other?

5. Would you like to know more about Nikki and Bone's history? If so, why?

6. Do you think Nikki should carry the baby to full term? If so, why or why not?

7. How can Nikki keep the baby from experiencing the same feelings of being raised with no father?

8. Do you think Nikki was rejecting her stepfather, Benny Harris, or did he project his animosity for Terry onto Nikki causing her to feel a difference in the atmosphere?

9. Should Nikki investigate further into Magic's disappearance and raise their child as a single parent?

10. Do you think Wendy knows a lot more and could have told Nikki what was coming down the pipeline?

11. Do you want to know who Nikki's dad is? What happened to him?

12. Should Terry have told Nikki about her father before the age of twenty? Could it have impacted Nikki's coping mechanisms?

If you find this fictional piece relatable, that's because fiction can mimic facts, just as fact is sometimes stranger than fiction. Hold on to your seats because the prequel BLAME IT BONE will give you more insight into the shenanigans of Hangtown.

www.ingramcontent.com/pod-product-compliance
Lightning Source LLC
Chambersburg PA
CBHW040838010826
48978CB00012BB/801